A CHRISTMAS DARE

HEATHER MIEKSTYN

I

To my husband, the best ice skater I know and my favorite romantic hero. Thanks for watching Christmas movies with me. But also- thanks for letting me watch some of them by myself.

xoxo,
   Heather

CONTENTS

CHAPTER ONE-CASSIE

Duster: slang hockey term for a player who doesn't get much playing time and collects dust on the bench

The December I turned eight years old, I announced to my mom that when I grew up, I was going to marry Santa Claus. Sitting here in a jail cell across from a guy in a musty, rented Santa Claus suit was not what I had in mind. Especially when the guy is Spencer Owens. The man I used to love. The man who broke my heart. The man I've spent the last five years trying to get over. The man I'd fooled myself into thinking I *was* over.

The fact that I'm now in jail with him proves that I was absolutely wrong about this. And isn't that just stab-a-snowman-with-a-carrot fantastic?

"You've got fingerprint ink on your skirt." Spence's deep voice startles me from this unsettling realization, and I look down at my green bell skirt to see he's right. There's a long black streak of ink down the right side of it. No way Layla's mom doesn't make me pay to replace this costume, even though it has to be as old as me, if not older. The elves at Evergreen Farm and Nursery's annual Christmas Wonderland have always worn this ridiculous green dress with the giant red belt cinched around the middle. The accompanying garish red and green striped tights and oversized

1

elf shoes that curve up at the toe really complete the festive look of the outfit. Not to mention the jingle bell hat. I sound like Santa's sleigh is swooping out of the sky towards you if I even so much as nod.

"Oh great." The sigh I let out is so heavy, it makes my hat jingle.

"I'd say you could order a new one before Mrs. Shanahan even notices it, but I doubt Amazon prime offers same day shipping all the way up here."

"Funny, Spencer. We're not that Podunk, you know. Amazon ships here."

"Right, sorry. Why don't you go online and order your elf costume now, that way she can have it by next Christmas."

I cross my arms across my chest, staring daggers at him. "Why did you even come back here Spence, if you hate Superior Falls so much."

"I don't hate Superior Falls, Cassie." Spencer scratches at his white Santa beard, finally pulling it off with a tug. I wish he hadn't. It was so much easier to hate him when I couldn't see his chiseled jawline. "It's just..."

"Alright you two," another voice, this one belonging to the sheriff, interrupts Spencer before I get to hear how he was going to finish that sentence. I have a guess though. He doesn't hate Superior Falls, he just hasn't come back in five years because of me. I'm here. A blatant reminder of his ugly past. "Now, I know the pair of you don't want to spend Christmas Eve sleeping in a jail cell, so start talking." Sheriff Tom stands there, arms crossed over his chest, waiting expectantly for us to explain ourselves.

"Tom, nothing they can say can get them out of this." His deputy Vince walks into the room, shooting a nasty look at Spencer. "They were caught red-handed trying to steal a Christmas tree off the farm. This is the fifth time this month a tree has been stolen. We've finally caught the perps. Although I am surprised to see Santa still has so many clothes on after all the ones he's left behind around the farm this month." Vince laughs at his own joke, a nod to the tree thief's calling card of leaving various parts of a Santa suit in place of the trees they've taken.

"Aw c'mon Vince!" Spencer steps up to the bars. "You can't honestly think Cass and I are the Evergreen Bandits. I told you when you drove up, we left cash by the register."

"Sounds like a cock and bull story to me," Vince sneers. "I may not have thought Cassie was capable of this sort of crime, but I have no doubts where you're concerned. Too bad your professional hockey player status won't help you here, Slick."

Spencer doesn't even blink. "Don't take out your unlived dreams on me, duster."

"Please," Vince scoffs, "I'm perfectly happy with my life choices. I'm not the one sitting in a jail cell in a Santa suit. What's your coach going to say when he finds out about this Owens? I heard he's a real stickler for the rules. Doesn't take kindly to his players breaking them."

"Do you want to hear our side of the story or not?" Spencer looks at Tom, ignoring Vince's jab, but my interest is peaked. Has getting arrested really put Spence's career at risk? The man lives and breathes hockey. Always has, always will. A spasm of remorse moves through me. What if I messed that up for him?

"Alright you two, just calm down," Tom speaks up again, holding out his hands between them like the iron bars might not be sufficient. "Vince, I know you have a vendetta against Owens here, but we're officers of the law, we have to put aside personal feelings, and do what's right. Now if Owens said he left money by the cash register, maybe we ought to check."

"What does it matter if he did?" Vince cries. "They were still trespassing. You want to buy a Christmas tree, do it during regular business hours like the rest of us."

"We couldn't," I finally speak. "We were busy working during regular business hours. Employees aren't allowed to make purchases while working."

"Oh yeah, I forgot Owens came home to do some charity work for his sweet little grandma." Vince laughs, the act marring his normally handsome features. "And now he's going to end up staying home to do additional charity work. This time in the form of court ordered community service."

"Enough!" Tom's voice is hard now. "Vince, I'm going to head back over to the tree farm and see if I can verify their story about the cash. I'd send you, but at this point I'm not sure I can trust you to tell the truth. I want you to go back to manning the front desk. Leave these two alone. I'm going to try calling Molly Shanahan again. See if I can't get her down here. Whatever you think Vince, I can't say I see these two being the Evergreen Bandits. There's something else going on here, and I'm going to find out what."

"C'mon Tom," Vince starts to protest, but Tom shuts him down with a glare. With one last dirty look at Spence, Vince stalks off, slamming the door behind him.

"Alright you two," Tom sticks his hat back on his head, "I'll be back shortly. Even if I do find cash though, Vince is right that this still leaves you with a potential trespassing charge. You'd better hope I can get ahold of Molly Shanahan to vouch for you, or you'll likely be sitting in here all night."

CHAPTER TWO-SPENCER

Chassé: (pronounced chă-say) a basic
dance step used in figure skating

I should never have come back. That's the thought that skitters to a landing in my brain as the door closes behind Tom. I could be safely tucked away in bed inside my Manhattan brownstone. Instead, I'm in a jail cell in Superior Falls. At home my bed has 800 thread count sheets. To be honest, I don't actually care about thread count. I only mention it, because here in this jail cell, the bed has no sheet. Thread count: zero. That's right, it's just a bare mattress. A bare mattress with far too many suspicious stains on it for me to even think about going near it.

Behind me Cassie sighs, and I turn around to see her sinking back onto the metal bench against the wall. She kneads her hand along her ankle, and while I know that she's not trying to make me feel guilty, guilt stabs me nonetheless. Guilt has been my constant companion the last five years though, so it's no surprise he makes his presence louder here in the town where he first arrived on the scene of my life.

"You, uh, need ice or something?" I gesture to her leg, and she immediately stops her movements, placing her hands back in her lap. I'm disturbed by the fact that I still find her so gorgeous, even wearing that ugly, outdated elf costume. Even when I know I don't deserve her anymore. Didn't ever, really.

"No, it's fine." She avoids my eyes. "I'm fine."

"Right." I look around the cell, desperate for some sort of distraction. I've been in here all of twenty minutes and already I'm thinking of going Shawshank on this place and trying to dig my way out. I bet I could use the prong on this Santa belt to scratch off the days spent here. Or possibly the minutes.

"So," Cassie's voice comes out in a nervous squeak. She clears her throat and tries again. "So, is your coach really going to be mad at you about this? Because maybe I could talk to him. Try and explain. It was my fault, after all."

I stare at her for a minute. "You want to talk to Darren Reynolds?" I finally say.

"Sure." Cassie nods. "If it would help."

Only Cassie Whitley would think it was no big deal to call up an NHL coach she's never met. A man whose nickname in the league is The Beast, thanks to his legendary snarl and tendency to throw things. He's a great coach, but there's not a warm or fuzzy bone in his body. He would chew Cassie up and spit her out if she tried to call and explain why exactly she and I got arrested for stealing a Christmas tree. No way am I letting her anywhere near the man.

"I can handle my coach," I finally tell her. "But thanks for the offer."

More silence follows this pronouncement, and I tug at my belt, thinking once again about tally marks along the wall.

"You can sit if you want." Cassie gestures to the bench. "I can scooch down." The bench is about six feet long. There's more than enough room for two people, yet she's looking at me like she might get cooties if I dare sit too close. I'm more worried about getting cooties from that bare mattress though, so I take her up on the offer and sit down. She automatically shifts further away down the bench. We're magnets with the same pole, repelling each other and creating friction.

Once upon a time, I had the opposite effect on her. Where I went, she went, and vice versa. We were two magnets violently attracted to each other. Until the accident. I shudder involuntarily at the memory. Cassie, always observant, notices.

"Don't tell me it's too cold in this cell for the hockey player?" Her nose crinkles in amusement, an expression I recognize. An expression I've missed. "Especially one dressed as Santa."

"Funny Cassie-Chassé," her old nickname slides off my tongue, before I can stop it. "But I'm not cold," I add quickly, hoping to skate over my gaffe.

Her amusement vanishes. "Don't call me that Spencer."

Guilt roars back to full attention. "Right, sorry."

Cassie stands, pacing the length of the cell like I'm not even here.

"I was fine, you know," she finally says, coming to a stop right in front of me. "After you left. I was fine. I *am* fine. So don't sit there and feel sorry for me."

"I-I don't feel sorry for you," I stammer.

"Good." Her eyes are on fire with anger, and I know I should say something else, but I'm too mesmerized by those eyes. Two blue blazes aimed directly at me. I should run before I get burned, but instead I move towards the flames, standing up off the bench so we're only inches apart.

"Spencer, don't," her voice is laced with warning, but I'm in too deep now.

"Cassie," her name breathes out of me like a whisper in a cave, filling the space, then echoing back until it's all I hear, until she's all I see. "I've missed you." What would she do if I kissed her right now? I want to kiss her. In my memories, the ones I fall asleep to every night, I can still taste her lips on mine. Strawberries and mint. Sweet and refreshing. Like the mist of a waterfall hitting your skin on a hot day.

"You're the one who left Spencer," her answering whisper breaks the spell, and I step back, ashamed at having almost lost control. She's right. I'm the one who left. I didn't deserve her then, and I don't deserve her now. I just need to get out of this jail cell, then hightail it back to New York before I do any more damage to her life.

CHAPTER THREE-CASSIE

**Double Dog Dare: An intensified form of a dare.
Frequently used after the dared person initially
refuses. For further reference, see "Triple Dog Dare".**

I can't believe I almost kissed him! The guy I used to love. The guy who broke my heart. The guy...oh wait, already been over all that. Instead of thinking about Spencer, I try to focus on my breathing, since apparently my seething anger has the same sound effect as a rhino on the run. Super hot. Not that I care about how I look in front of Spencer. I do not. Much.

If I did, would I still be wearing this ridiculous elf costume? Granted it's that or my, uh, undergarments. But still.

Anyway, where was I? Oh yes, I was seething. And also, actively ignoring the heat that's been pooling in my stomach ever since Spencer's lips hovered only inches from mine. Ever since he arrived back in town really. But it's been a fairly mild December for northern Michigan, so the heat thing is probably down to that.

"I'm sorry, Cass," Spencer says for the hundredth time tonight. "Muscle memory just took over or something."

"Muscle memory?" I snort. "Oh good. Glad to know you didn't actually *want* to kiss me, it was just a reflex. You sure know how to waltz into town and flatter a girl."

"Cassie," his voice is a growl now. I tell myself I do not find this sexy.

"Spencer," I hiss back, finally letting myself look at him. He's leaning against the cell bars, arms over his chest, legs crossed at the ankle. Basically, he's managing to pull off the whole bad boy archetype even though he's wearing a Santa suit. Well ho-ho-ho for him.

"You'd better let me back there, Vincent Pacini!" Layla's outraged voice slams through the wall separating us from the front desk, breaking our staredown. "You think I don't have your mother on speed dial? I will call her, and I will tell her what really happened to her car junior year."

"Alright, alright. Geez, Layla," Vince grumbles. "Don't blow your top."

I hear the scrape of his chair against the wooden floor, then a second later the door opens, and Layla appears.

"Oh my gosh, Cassie!" Layla comes running towards me, shaking the bars like there's a chance her emotions might give her hulk strength, so she can bust me out of here. "Let her out, Vince! Let her out now!" She whirls around to face him. "Where are your keys?" She holds out her hand expectantly. "Gimme."

"I'm not giving you my keys, Layla." Vince puts his hand protectively to his belt loop, where the keys jangle.

"This is all your fault." Now she turns her wrath on Spencer.

"I told my mom we shouldn't let you be Santa, but she was all, having a famous hockey player as our Santa will bring so much business to the farm, Layla. You know we need that right now." She imitates her mother's no-nonsense tone, even sticking her hand on her hip the same way Molly always does. "I guess I was right this time."

"Yeah, well don't worry. I won't offer my services again," Spence says with a sigh. "I only came back because my grandma said it was important. I didn't realize she had such a soft spot for your farm. I didn't even know that Cas-" He stops himself from finishing the sentence, shaking his head. "Whatever, it doesn't matter. I'll be on the next bus out of town once I get out of this cell. You won't hear from me again."

This should make me happy, so why does my heart plummet to the floor at his words?

"Good," Layla's eyes are narrowed almost to slits, "because Spencer, Cassie doesn't want you here. Okay?"

His eyes flit to mine, a strange sadness evident in the green of his irises. My mouth opens, then shuts as I swallow down the words of denial on the tip of my tongue. I won't tell him to stay. I tried that once before, and it didn't work. The pain his leaving etched into me is too deep, no matter what I said to him about being fine. There is still so...much...hurt. I'd buried it under other things these past five years, but his reemergence has it clawing its way back to the surface. Raw and fresh and somehow even more painful than the first time around.

"Here, here," Vince pipes up. "Finally something you and I agree on Layla."

"Got the message," Spencer says with a grunt, before turning and walking to the corner of the cell where he resumes his impression of James Dean.

"I called my mom Cass," Layla addresses me again. "She's on her way. Obviously, she won't press charges. But girl, what were you doing taking a tree? None of this makes sense." She shifts her gaze to Spencer. "Did he put you up to it? Some sort of dare from the big-time hockey player? Let's mess with the small-town Christmas tree farm just for kicks and giggles?"

I just stare at her, unable to bring myself to tell her the truth. I didn't even tell Spencer the whole truth, and he was in that forest with me, running the blade of the saw back and forth along the tree bark. My mind travels back over the last month, replaying the days on triple speed, like I've just hit the time lapse button on my phone's camera.

Molly's announcement that if this tree season didn't go well, they may have to close the farm. Me volunteering to be an elf for their Christmas Wonderland in an attempt to help offset some of the operating costs of the farm. The discovery that a tree had been stolen, the remaining stump covered with a Santa hat. Less than a week later, a family of four rushing over to the checkout kiosk to tell Layla they'd found a tree stump with Santa's distinctive gold-buckled belt wrapped around it. Another tree had been stolen. The subsequent front page news article broadcasting the news. The uptick in business at the farm thanks to the sensational story. Who wouldn't want to buy their Christmas tree from the farm where Santa is supposedly stealing Christmas trees for his own personal use?

The next stump had Santa's boots on it. The one after that his pants. That discovery had garnered another story in the news, because obviously everyone found it hilarious. There was even a whole slew of memes and gifs that came out of that one. *Santa drops trou at the local Christmas tree farm* and all that. Business boomed.

And I thought nothing of it. So stupid.

"Hello! Cassie?" Layla weaves her hand through the bar and gives me a poke. "Where you at? The North Pole?" She giggles at her own joke.

"It was me." Spencer surprises me, rising from his corner to approach us. "You got it right, Layla. It was one of our stupid dares. Me trying to relive Cassie and I's high school glory days."

Liar. Why is he lying? My breath catches in my throat as the answer settles in my chest. For me. He's lying for me. But why? He can't possibly still care about me. You don't vanish out of someone's life for five years to go live out your dreams because you care about them. You do that because you care about yourself.

"I knew it!" Layla scowls. "And now you've probably distracted Tom and Vince from finding the real Evergreen Bandits because they're too wrapped up with you two. Didn't you learn your lesson the last time one of your dares ended badly? Messing up Cassie's entire future didn't turn you off the whole double-dog dare idiocy?"

My whole body flushes. Like I'm pretty sure my belly button is red. My kneecaps? Tomato red. Between my toes? Redder than a fire engine.

"I guess not." Spencer's voice is tight, but he doesn't flinch. I do. Because Layla's accusations and Spencer's admissions…they're just all part of yet another lie. This one both of ours. No, this one just mine. Spencer and I may share in the original subterfuge, but I was the one that let it continue after he left. The one that didn't have enough courage to tell the truth. It's just me, Spencer, and God that know what actually happened on that night five years ago.

"Layla, stop." I can't handle all of this anymore, the truth suddenly feels like lava bubbling up inside me, preparing to erupt. "Please." Oh no, I think I'm crying. Salt slides into my mouth. Yup. I'm definitely crying.

"Look what you did?" This time Layla's hand snakes through the bars to slug Spencer on the shoulder.

Spencer doesn't answer. He doesn't even seem to register that she's spoken, let alone that she punched him. He steps towards me, agony drawn across his face. He looks down at me, using his broad body to shield me from Layla and Vince's curious gazes.

"It's okay," he mouths to me, his hands coming up to wipe the tears from my cheeks. The contact feels like that first burst of sunshine after you've stepped out an over-air-conditioned building. Warm and welcome.

I'm still processing my body's response, when suddenly his lips are by my ear, sending a whole new surge of sensations down my spine. "I can take Layla harping on me, Cass. Don't worry about it. I only care about you. I've only ever cared about you."

And just like that, my tears stop. Because once again, he's the liar.

CHAPTER FOUR-SPENCER

Spence-I've thought about your proposal, and I think if other people want to join in on our Dare War, we should let them. But my dad CANNOT find out I'm behind it. He'd kill me if he knew. So my involvement as one of the Dare Masters needs to be anonymous.
 -Cassie

Cassie-No biggie on my end. My grandma thinks our dares are great fun. Her words, not mine. So at the end of the day, if we get caught, I don't mind taking the blame. Also, Dare Masters? I like it. We still get to play though, right?
 -Spence

Spence-I thought it had a nice ring to it. Better than Dare Mistress for sure, so let's just think of Master as a gender-neutral term. And OBVIOUSLY we still get to play! Playing will help us maintain our anonymity.

I've got a dare in mind for Layla Shanahan. See the enclosed dare note I typed up for her. Can you deliver it?

  -Cassie

Layla- Welcome to Lake Superior Middle School's Dare War! The rules are as follows (these can also be found on Twitter @LSMSDareWar):

1. **Dare must be completed within 48 hours of receiving your dare note.**
2. **Failure to complete your dare, will result in your elimination from Dare War.**

3. Dares are each worth a total of 10 points. Points are deducted for sloppiness, getting caught, and poor sportsmanship. The person with the highest total at the end of the school year wins.
4. Occasionally Double-Dog Dares will be posted on our social media account. These are worth double the points and go to the first person to claim them.
5. No parental involvement.
6. Snitches get stitches. Ha! Just kidding, but any hint that you've ratted out a participant and you will be eliminated from both this Dare War and any future Dare Wars held.

7. Take a picture of your dare and post it to our private social media account to receive your points.

For your first dare, we dare you to cover all of Mrs. Fritz's cheesy motivational posters with One Direction Posters.

Good luck!
-The Dare Masters

One second, I'm baring my soul the way I've dreamed about doing for the last 1,986 days since I first left Superior Falls, (That's right, I kept track. I may have been joking about making tally marks on the cell wall, but there's nothing funny about the journal I write in every day. There's a tally mark in there for each and every day that's gone by without seeing Cassie. Sure, some people might wonder what business a six foot three, two-hundred-and-ten-pound hockey player has keeping a journal, but there's nothing they can say that a full body check into the boards won't shut up.) and the next second Cassie is slapping me. Hard. And despite her tiny size, somehow it hurts more than the time that guy from the Red Wings slammed so hard into me, that I ended up in the hospital overnight for observation.

"Well, that slap was five years in the making," Layla crows from behind me, and I bite back the urge to snarl. Layla and I used to be friends back in high school, but it's clear where her allegiance currently lies. Does it matter that she participated in her fair share of the dares she referred to with so much disgust? Apparently not. I can still picture her face as she ran out of our high school after I dared her to break into the captain of the football's team gym locker and steal his cup. Yep, that kind of cup. And yes, that football captain was Vince. Possibly there's a reason the guy doesn't like me. Though really it started with the fact that he couldn't cut it as a hockey player, and he always hated that I could. I just responded to his dislike of me with dislike of my own. What can I say? I was a teenager.

As for Vince's dislike of me now, I have a pretty big inkling that it has less to do with my hockey success and more to do with the fact that he wants Cassie. The very thought of the two of them together brings up another snarl.

"Don't tell me you care about me." Cassie ignores Layla, her face inches from mine as she whispers venom at me. "You don't leave the people you care about."

I'm floored by her words. Doesn't she get it? "Cassie," the words tumble out of me, inadequate, but needing to be said, "I left *because* I cared about you. Because I wanted what was best for you. Because you-"

"Alright, enough fighting you two." Vince raps on the bars, the sound reverberating around the cell. "I don't want to have to cuff you to keep you in check." He smirks. "Not that I'd mind seeing you in cuffs, Owens."

"Keep your fantasies to yourself, Pacini," the retort slips out automatically, a casualty of years spent ribbing with teammates in the locker room. I hear a laugh burst out of Layla, but she promptly cuts it off. I shake my head, putting my attention back on Cassie. I don't want to engage in petty bickering with Vince. There's too much I have to say to Cassie.

"I hope I get to testify against you in court, you know that man." Vince scowls. "Layla, your time in here is up. You wanna get Cassie out, get your mom here. Believe me, I'd be happy to leave Owens in here all by himself. Cassie didn't deserve to have her life ruined by him back then, and she doesn't deserve it now either." He puffs up his chest, eyes on her. I can't help the way my hands curl into fists in response. "Like I've always tried to tell you Cassie, not all men are losers like Owens, here. Maybe after this you'll finally see that." Vince tugs Layla by the arm, guiding her out of the room.

"I'll be back Cass," Layla calls as she reluctantly follows him. "Don't worry. We'll get you out of here!"

Taking a deep breath I face Cassie, really ready this time to say what I've been holding in all these years. But as soon as my eyes find hers, she gets a panicked look on her face, then bolts for the cell door.

"Vince! Wait!" she cries desperately, making both him and Layla pause in the doorway. Vince turns back to her, looking cocky as heck at hearing his name on her lips. "I...need go to the bathroom," she squeaks.

CHAPTER FIVE-CASSIE

Hoser: Hockey trash talk term used to call a person a loser. Originates from the fact that before Zambonis were created, the losing team had to hose off the ice after the game.

As soon as the bathroom door closes behind me, I lean back against the door and attempt to do some of the breathing techniques my therapist taught me to help with the panic attacks I kept having after the accident. My legs are shaking so badly though, that I can't focus, and my deep breaths start to sound more like a woman in labor than anything remotely calming.

Having Spencer back in Superior Falls is completely messing with the new normal I've established. For so long we were inseparable, two halves of the same whole. Then I got hurt, and he left. Now he's trying to tell me he left for me? FOR me? Is he insane? And why is there a part of me that actually wants to hear what else he has to say? I guess I'm insane too.

I'm basically torn between Gloria Gaynor-ing him (you know, one hand on my hip, one slicing through the air as I tell him to just turn around, he's not welcome anymore, and so on) and attempting to be the Penelope to his Odysseus (I waited for you for five years, I said no to other suitors, now let's be us again). I think it must just be our history that's messing with me. How can I just erase the fourteen years of friendship that led us to the night of the accident?

I met Spencer when we were just two four-year-olds in our first learn to skate class. Rather than saying hi to me he greeted me with two words, "Knock, knock."

I gamely replied, "Who's there?"

He grinned wickedly and said, "Butt." I burst out laughing, firmly cementing our friendship. Over the next year, we continued to take skating classes together. Then, after we had both turned five, we begged my parents and his grandmother to let us try hockey. Together we began both kindergarten and hockey, as intertwined as two hockey sticks fighting for the same puck.

Then came the 2006 winter Olympics. I watched in complete awe as Sasha Cohen completed five triple jumps over the course of the games. I wanted to jump like that. Soar through the air gracefully and land with a winning smile. Have the audience throw roses at me. Wear those gorgeous outfits. So, I dropped hockey and took up figure skating.

Spencer gave me a hard time, teasing me for the toe pick on my new skates and telling me in typical seven-year-old boy fashion that he wasn't going to be friends with someone who wore frilly froufrou leotards.

That was when the dares started.

Stung by his rejection I told him the only reason he was being such a butthead was because he knew that in truth boys just weren't as tough as girls. If they were, they wouldn't have to go out on the ice in all their warm gear. Girls were WAY tougher, they could handle the cold in just their, ahem, frilly froufrou leotards. I went on to say that if he thought hockey and skates without toe picks were so much better then he should prove it. Then I dared him to go to his next hockey practice in just his boxers and a t-shirt. Spoiler alert: he did it.

He also got suspended from a week of hockey practices, but he never questioned our friendship or my toughness again. At least, not until after the accident. After the accident, he decided all on his own that I wasn't strong enough to get through my injury and the devastating effect it had on the course of my life. So, he left.

The ironic thing was, that in reality, I was strong enough to handle all of that. I just wasn't strong enough to get over him. Even if I did stand in front of the mirror hundreds of times singing "Stronger" by Britney Spears. I may have been a baby when that song came out, but somehow that anthem found me during those dark days. Pretty sure Molly Shanahan had some involvement in that.

The mirror in the bathroom catches my eyes, and I take a step towards it, studying my reflection with hollow eyes. "Stronger," I mouth to myself, then I add a little dance move, because hello,

87 percent of what was awesome about Britney were her dance moves. Sadly, nobody looks good dancing in an elf dress, but I persevere anyway, changing some of the lyrics to fit the situation.

"I don't need you, Spencer, better off alone. But there you go, you want me back." I lift my shoulder to my chin and give my reflection a saucy grin, because here in the privacy of this bathroom, I've got confidence. I can flirt...with myself. Not important. Restarting pep talk.

"Cassandra Whitley," I drop the singing, ready to get down to business, "you are going to go back out there, and you are going to give that man slash cretin the cold shoulder until Layla's mom arrives. Then you're going to take Molly aside and make her explain what exactly she's been doing for the last month."

I shift my weight as I reply to myself, "You're so funny, Cassie." I wave my hand dismissively. "I don't believe for a second that you'll do any of that."

I move back to my other side, completely engrossed in this conversation I'm having with myself. "Yeah, you're probably right. After all, I don't have a confrontational bone in my body."

"Then maybe," other me replies with a mischievous smile, "I should double dog dare you to do it."

"Cassie," Vince bangs on the door, and I jump in fright. Embarrassment floods me. Has he been standing on the other side of the door this whole time? Oh sleigh bells. What if he heard me?

On the plus side, if he did, it might make him stop hitting on me all the time. "You almost done in there?"

Oh right. I'm supposed to be going to the bathroom.

"Just a second!" I turn to the door, then, because now that I think about it, I do kind of have to go, turn back and quickly use the facilities before washing my hands and exiting the bathroom.

Vince grins at me as I emerge. The same cocky sort of smarmy grin he always gives me. Guess he didn't hear me conversing with myself then. "You don't have to keep that thing on you know." Vince indicates my hat. "You're not working anymore." He reaches up and, before I can make a move to stop him, tugs the jingle bell hat off my head. The jangling of the bells as the hat leaves my head is so loud, Vince and I both cringe. Then my body goes into self-defense mode, and I yank the hat back from him, creating another crescendo of bell jingling. But it's too late, the paper, the one I was so safely hiding inside my hat, has already fallen to the floor. Vince sees it too. I make a mad grab for it, but it's closer to him, and his fingers close around it before mine even hit the floor.

"What's this Cassie?" Vince waves the paper teasingly over my head. Never before have I hated being short as much as I do in that moment.

"Vince, c'mon, give it back."

"Not until I read it." He shakes the paper open, still holding it out of my reach as he cricks his neck up to read it.

"Vince, seriously!" I jump as high as I can, but my hand doesn't even brush the paper. I feel like the weight on the pole of one of those ring the bell carnival games, moving up the pole but never getting close enough to actually ring that stupid bell and get the prize.

"Oh-ho," Vince crows, "this is gold, Cassie. Gold!" He pivots, taking quick strides back to the holding cell. "Wait till Owens hears this." He raises his voice. "Owens, you've clearly lost your game," he calls out to Spencer, laughing maniacally.

He doesn't even have to tell me to follow him, I'm already hot on his heels. "Do not show that to Spencer, Vince!" I paw ineffectually at his back. This is bad. So bad. Maybe I should make a run for it. At the very least doing so would divert Vince's attention back to me. I'm about to make my move when Vince starts reading, and horror freezes me in place.

"Ten Reasons I Want Nothing to do with Spencer Owens," Vince pauses, "the I is Cassie, in case you were wondering Owens." He smirks at Spencer, whose eyes are moving back and forth between Vince and I. He looks furious. Whether with me or Vince, I can't be sure.

"One." Vince holds up a finger. "His car. I do not miss driving in that thing. I mean, we get it ya hoser, you play hockey. That doesn't mean you have to store all your pads and gear in your backseat. Put them in the trunk for goodness sake. His car always smelled like a foot died in it." Vince guffaws, before moving on. My face is on fire.

"Two. Speaking of hockey. He plays it. Which makes him about a million times more likely to lose teeth than the average human. And nothing against people who are incisor-ly or bicuspid-ly challenged, but I prefer the men in my life to be fully toothed." Vince's mirth cannot be contained. He's slapping his leg he finds this so funny. Tears even leak out of the corners of his evil eyes. I want to shout at him. Tell him to stop reading. But I'm as mute as Ariel after she gave her voice to the sea witch. If he makes it to the last item on the list, the one I scribbled hastily on there earlier this afternoon, I will die. And my tombstone will read "EMBARRASSMENT KILLS". Hopefully Layla will start a Facebook group in memory of me or maybe host an annual Embarrassment Awareness fundraiser benefiting the youth of the town.

"Three." Vince has recovered from his laughing fit. "He's been in New York for five years now. He's probably become cold and heartless. I bet whenever he walks down Fifth Avenue or wherever, he doesn't smile or wave to anyone. Not to mention his lung capacity has likely decreased from all the air pollution there. And decreased lung capacity surely negatively affects one's kissing ability. Not that I want to kiss Spencer Owens, but still. Worth noting." Vince snorts. "Doubt Owens was ever much of a kisser, Cassie. Take me up on my offer to take you out to dinner, and I'll show you how good a kiss can be."

I barely hear this last part. My attention is too focused on Spencer. Up until Vince's last comment there'd been amusement playing on his lips. He'd found my list funny, maybe even heard it as encouragement. After all, why would I have written a list of reasons to stay away from him, unless I knew there'd be a part of me that didn't want to stay away from him? That's right, I wouldn't have. I have to get that list from Vince before he gets to number eleven. I jump up to where he's holding the list again, but Vince easily keeps it away from me, even going so far as to dangle the paper teasingly in front of me before removing it at the last second when I make a grab for it.

"Cut it out, Vince." Spencer's voice is deadly.

Vince ignores him, his eyes back on the list, reading the next few items on it. Letting my list fall to his side, he looks straight at me. "Maybe I've been going about this the wrong way though, Cassie. Instead of asking you to go out with me, maybe I should dare you." He steps even closer to me, and I resist the urge to shrink away from him. This is my chance to grab my list. I just have to wait for the right moment.

"Pacini, you better back off!" Spencer shakes the bars in frustration. "Get away from her!"

Again, Vince ignores him. He knows there's nothing Spencer can do to him thanks to the bars separating them. "You always were a sucker for a dare, Cassie. So, what do you say? I dare you to go out to dinner with me." He licks his lips. "No, I double-dog dare you." His eyes are hooded on mine. "And I promise the night won't end with you in a hospital bed like some other people's dares." He waggles his eyebrows. "Though we don't have to rule out a different type of bed."

Spencer's angry shout reverberates around the room as he cusses Vince out for disrespecting me. All good sense and reason float out the window in that moment, and my hand moves up of its own accord slapping him hard across the face. Great, now I've slapped two people tonight. One of them a police officer. That's right, I've assaulted an officer of the law! Oh gingersnaps. I'm going to be in jail for Christmas, aren't I? I hope Molly at least brings me a piece of her famous peppermint cheesecake.

"Sheez, Cassie!" Vince grabs his throbbing cheek. "What the heck?"

I should apologize. Possibly even agree to go out with him. Maybe then he won't press charges. "Don't talk about things you know nothing about," I hiss at him instead, because he's a jerk, and I refuse to take this crap from him. In one fluid motion I yank the paper from his hand and start tearing it to shreds. (Nobody panic—I have another copy at home.) The pieces drift to the floor like snow. Vince's face turns a putrid shade of pink. He grabs me by the arm, unlocks the cell door, and practically shoves me inside.

"Guess what, Cassie. I'm no longer interested. I don't date felons. And that's what you are now that you've assaulted an officer. I hope the pair of you rot in there this Christmas."

Without another word, Vince slams the door shut again and storms out. My breathing has gone erratic again at his words. Panic is clawing its way up my chest like an old familiar friend. I sink down unto the bench, putting my head between my knees, desperate for a full breath.

"Cassie." Spencer's voice is in my ear, and I almost clock him in the head as I whip around to see him sitting next to me, head bent low to be on level with mine. Concern is written all over his face. I should be embarrassed that I'm having a panic attack in front of him, but there's something so sweet about this giant man folding himself in half for me, that I just lock eyes with him, letting his presence sooth my anxiety.

CHAPTER SIX-SPENCER

Cassie's List of Christmas Expletives
(Created the December of Eighth Grade,
but still widely in use today)

1. *Oh my mistletoe!*
2. *Gingersnaps!*
3. *Oh sleigh bells!*
4. *Fa La La-Uck!*
5. *Shu-gar Cookie!*
6. *Jack Frost It!*
7. *Oh my snowball!*
8. *Holy hot cocoa!*
9. *Crinkle Cookie!*
10. *What the holly berry?*

Even as I sit next to Cassie on this tiny bench, trying to comfort her, fury is still running like fire through my veins. I want to bust my way out of this cell and find Vince, so I can pummel him. I hate the way he spoke to her. The insinuations he made about her. The fact that there was nothing I could do to stop him. The memory makes my skin crawl. But then Cassie's breathing hitches, and I focus back on her, trying to figure out how to help.

"What can I do?" I ask her worriedly, reaching out and taking her hand in mine. Warmth seeps through me when she doesn't push my hand away. It could just be that she's in the middle of a panic attack and is too engrossed in trying to work through that to push me away, but for now I'm going to take it as a positive sign. Especially if you pair it with that list. You don't make a list like that if you don't have at least some lingering feelings for a guy, right? I wish I could've seen the rest of the list before she tore it up. Not that I would want slimy Vince to be the one reading it to me. No, I'd prefer my own personal copy, which I'd take straight to the local stationary store to be laminated.

"I'm," Cassie breathes, "sorry."

"Don't apologize." If she weren't struggling to breath, I'd actually be enjoying this moment. Her hand in mine, the smell of her vanilla shampoo filling my senses, the memory of that list of hers. My eyes go to the torn-up slips of paper on the floor. Again I wonder what else the list said. I've always loved Cassie's lists. Even if I did use to tease her about them. "How can I help you?" I ask again.

"I need to get out of my head," she tells me, her voice rasping. "Can you just talk to me." Her eyes dart to my face, still only inches from hers. "But not about us," she adds, before sticking her head back between her knees. "Tell me about New York. Hockey. Your life." Her voice breaks a little on that last word, and I cringe.

"New York," I repeat, "is, uh, large." Lame. So lame. I try again. "I mean, obviously most places seem large compared to Superior Falls, but you know you just can't picture how tall a skyscraper is until you've actually seen one up close. They're crazy high up, you know?" Worse. Somehow worse. I clear my throat. I used to be able to talk to this woman for hours. Now I'm a pathetic mess. "The, uh, food is good," I continue. "Bagels and stuff."

That's when the laughter starts. At first, I think she just hiccupped, but then another sound escapes her lips, and I realize she's trying to hold in laughter. Panic attack over then?

"I'm sorry," this time her breathing issues are related to how hard she's laughing. She sits up fanning her face as tears of mirth slide down her cheeks. "It's just. Bagels and stuff? Skyscrapers? Those are your takeaways from New York City?"

"Hey," I say indignantly, enjoying the way her cheeks have turned rosy from laughter, "the bagels are really good." I sit up too. "Besides, you flustered me with your whole," I wave my hand over her, "I can't breathe thing." And your general presence, I add silently. "On the plus side, it seems like that's over."

She stops laughing. "You're right." Her voice is full of wonder.

"I know. Clearly my asinine conversational skills helped."

"I guess so." She offers me a glimmer of a smile. I want to know what I can do to make her beam.

"Does this sort of thing happen a lot?" I ask her tentatively.

"Uh, it used to." Cassie avoids my gaze. "In the months after my injury it happened a lot. So, my mom started having me see a therapist to help me work through everything that happened." Her blue eyes finally rise to meet mine. "Guess I'm not as strong as you always thought I was."

"Cassie," I'm stunned by her words, "having panic attacks has nothing to do with strength. If anything, the fact that you have them and are able to work through them makes you stronger."

"Maybe." Cassie shrugs. "But I wasn't just talking about my panic attacks. I've shown a lot of weakness over the years."

I rub my cheek where she slapped me not too long ago. "I don't know, Vince and I can both attest that you've got a mean right slap."

Cassie laughs. "Yeah, sorry about that."

"Really?" I raise skeptical eyebrows her way.

Before she can answer Tom reappears. "Okay you two. At least one part of your story checks out. We did find a wad of cash by the register with a note that said 'For the Tree', but that doesn't explain away the other four trees that have gone missing. Now Owens, you were out of town for those other robberies, but Cassie, unfortunately, you can't say the same. I'd like to take you to our interview room so we can chat about those nights."

"Oh," Cassie's face pales, "right."

"Hold on," I stand, automatically putting a hand on Cassie's shoulder, "Does she have to go? She's not legally obligated to speak with you."

"Uh, true," Tom taps his foot impatiently on the floor, "but if she's not guilty then what does she have to lose?"

I look down at Cassie. Her eyes are two balls of terror. Wait... Is she guilty? I can't believe that. Earlier tonight she told me this was a one off. That she just wanted to get a tree and take it to one of her skating student's homes for the holidays. She said the little girl's dad had lost his job, and they hadn't been able to afford a tree this year. Was that a lie? Or had she stolen all of the other trees for similar reasons? Was she acting as some sort of Christmas version of Robin Hood? Stealing trees from the farm to give to the poor?

I don't have time to ask Cassie any of these questions, because she's already standing up to go with Tom. I squeeze her hand as she walks by me, but she doesn't look at me. Just steps through the cell door and follows Tom out of the room. I wish I had asked if I could go with them. I wish I had never left her alone in the first place.

CHAPTER SEVEN-CASSIE

Spence-I think my brain is atrophying. Seriously, what are the chances Mr. Jenkins is attempting to kill us all with this lesson? I will eat my own foot if I ever have to use the periodic table outside of this class. On the plus side, I've had plenty of time to come up with an epic dare for you. It's so good, I think you'll want to do it yourself, rather than passing it on to some other lucky recipient. I dare you to sneak into Principal Mack's office and switch out his PA microphone with that voice changer microphone you got from your grandma's white elephant gift exchange last month. The voice setting you want to use is up to you, but I'm partial to the Batman one. The

Helium setting is a close second
though. Have fun!
♡
  -Cassie

**Cassie Chassé-Oh yeah, this one's all me.
Batman today. Helium tomorrow, baby.**

   -Spence

As I sit down across the table from Sheriff Tom, I discreetly wipe my palms on my elf skirt. Maybe I should've just refused to come back here, like Spencer suggested. Or at least asked for a lawyer to be present. But I don't need a lawyer. I just need to talk to Molly.

"Alright Cassie," Tom settles himself in the chair across from me and gives me a kind smile, "no need to look so worried. I know it's scary being in a police interrogation room, but innocent people have nothing to fear while they're in here." He laughs at his rhyme. "Well, well. I'm a policeman and a poet, and I didn't even know it!"

Even though this isn't funny, I laugh. The man is questioning me about a crime! If he insisted that the sky was green, I'd agree with him. It's all about putting your best foot forward. Especially when your foot is only mostly innocent. What's the penalty for withholding information about a crime to a police officer again? Gosh, why don't they play episodes of *Law and Order* in here?

"First things first." Tom rubs his hands together, all business now that he's established his poetic ways. "Where were you the night of December 11? That being the night the first tree was stolen."

"December 11?" I rack my brain, doing some mental math to figure out that was a Sunday. Sundays are usually Husky game days. That's right. You caught me. I watch Spencer's games. If you grew up with someone who is now a professional athlete,

41

obviously you'd have at least some interest in their career. For instance, if you knew they were playing hockey at the University of Michigan, one of the top schools that pro hockey players get drafted from, obviously you'd watch the draft each summer to see if they were going to get picked up. And when the New York Huskies, the newest NHL team, put that person that you grew up with on their roster, you'd obviously watch their first game. And all 234 of their subsequent games. Obviously, you would. Right? Oh my mistletoe, I can't believe I thought I was over him. I am such an idiot.

"Cassie?" Tom is still waiting for my answer.

"Sorry, just thinking," I scramble for my reply, "Uh, I had a learn to skate class late that afternoon, then I went home. Watched some TV." No need to mention what I was watching. "Turned in early."

"Can anyone verify that?"

"Um. My learn to skate parents can verify that I taught class that day."

"Okay, but I'm actually more interested in your whereabouts between 8 p.m. and 6 a.m. That's the window for the tree robberies."

"Right." I chew my lower lip. The truth is I have no alibi. It's not like my TV can vouch for me. I may have a smart TV, but it's not *that* smart. The other truth is, I know who did it. And it wasn't me.

But I also can't let that person get caught. That's the whole reason I decided to steal a tree tonight. I wanted to get caught. Make people think I'm the one whose been stealing trees this whole time. So why am I freezing up now? This is what I wanted. Molly won't press charges, especially when she realizes why I did this. It's all to protect her. The woman who's been more like a mom to me these last five years than my own mother. Still, my plan seems so foolish here in this interrogation room with Vince's threat about charging me for assaulting an officer hanging over my head. Everything has gotten out of hand.

"Cassie?" Tom prompts me again. "Do you have anyone who can vouch for your whereabouts on the night of December 11?"

"Uh, no," I admit. I try to swallow, but my throat has gone dry. "I was alone."

"Okay." Tom nods, looking down at his clipboard. "How about December 15? You got an alibi for that robbery? Or the nineteenth? Or the twenty-second? If you have an alibi for even one of those nights it would really help you out Cassie. Especially since we caught you red-handed tonight. Of course, you and Owens don't seem to have followed the usual MO of the Evergreen Bandit. He or she has never left payment before. Plus, I sent one of my guys to search the farm, and I haven't found any, uh," his lips fight a smile, "discarded Santa clothing on any of the tree stumps."

Jack Frost It! I totally forgot to leave any clothing behind on the tree we took. I even had a beard sitting in my truck's glove box that I'd intended to leave. But Spencer's insistence on helping me with the tree threw me for a loop. I'd never meant for him to get involved, but then he saw me grabbing a saw after closing and asked what I was doing. In a panic I made up a story about wanting to cut a tree down for one of my underprivileged skating students. After that he refused to take no for an answer. "You can't cut down and transport an entire Douglas Fir by yourself Cassie," he kept saying. Worn out from a day spent watching him be the world's best Santa, I gave in and let him come. (I mean, the man had not only given each child his full attention as they spouted seven-minute-long run-on sentences about all of their Christmas wishes, he'd also been gracious enough to sign autographs for each eager, but slightly bashful dad that came forward with a hockey stick or a skate. Basically, I'd been trying to silence my uterus the entire day. We do not want to have this man's babies, you traitor. Stop ovulating immediately! And so on.)

"The other thing that confuses me," he goes on, "is how you would have done those other robberies by yourself. Owens wasn't around to help you then and, no offense, but you're about as big as my thigh. I can't see you moving a seven-foot sixty-pound tree by yourself."

"I'm stronger than I look," I say before I can stop myself. I've gotten this far into my plan, I can't chicken out now. Anyway, Tom and Spencer are on about how I couldn't move a tree by myself, but if Molly could move the other four trees by herself, then surely I could move one lousy tree on my own...Unless she had an accomplice? The idea freezes my veins. Did Layla help her? Has my best friend been in on this the whole time without me knowing? I think back over the last few days.

I'd first gotten suspicious a few days ago, when Molly burst in on Layla and I doing each other's nails in their kitchen, announcing with excitement that she had a celebrity Santa planned for the farm's Christmas Eve Santa's Village. She'd refused to tell us who it was, and seemed to avoid eye contact with me as she dodged our interrogations. I should've known then that it was Spencer. Which other celebrity would Molly Shanahan, born and raised here in Superior Falls, have access to?

She had a garment bag tucked in her arms. And when she wouldn't tell us which celebrity was coming to Superior Falls, I moved on to what she had in that bag. "Do you have a fancy date you haven't told us about Molly?" I teased her. I took her answering blush as a yes, at least until she walked out of the kitchen a few minutes later, and I got a glimpse of red velvet poking out of the bottom, a section of white fur caught in the zipper. The velvet was lined with a distinctive sheer gold silk material. It was that gold silk that caught my attention. The only Santa suit lined with gold silk that I knew of, was the one owned by Evergreen Tree Farm and Nursery. But why was Molly bringing home the farm's Santa suit?

In all the time I'd known the Shanahan's, the Santa suit had never left the farm. Layla once told me that when the Shanahan's started the farm almost seventy years ago, her great-grandfather had been Santa at the first Christmas Wonderland. The farm's roaring success that year had often been attributed to his performance. He in turn had attributed his performance to the magic of the suit. More precisely, the secret gold silk lining his wife had sewn into the suit. The lining that not only kept him extra warm and cozy, but made him feel like dancing. The people, he'd always said with a roaring laugh, loved a dancing Santa.

Over the years the suit had become a family heirloom, passed down from father to son. At least until Layla's parents, Molly and Ricky, got married and only had one daughter- Layla. For a long time, it hadn't mattered. Most of the Shanahan men played Santa until they were in their late fifties or early sixties before passing it unto one of their sons anyway. But then six years ago, Ricky died in a car accident. Grief stricken, Molly hadn't even run Christmas Wonderland that year. The following year, Ricky's sister Jenny had begged her husband Pete to play Santa. Begrudgingly he'd done so, but some of the magic seemed to have gone out of the operation. Pete had even insisted on bringing his own Santa suit, disgusted at the thought of wearing a seventy-year-old suit. Pete was a one and done Santa, so the following year Molly had hired the position out, and she'd done so ever since. Unable to bear the thought of a non-Shanahan wearing the magic family suit, she'd simply kept it stored at the farm, hidden away in the staff room.

Unfortunately, the farm's sales had been going steadily down since Ricky's death. Though a huge portion of this could be attributed to economic recession in the area and a few bouts of extreme weather that affected the crop of trees, Molly was often heard saying that the farm had lost its Christmas magic the day Ricky died. It hadn't been until the beginning of this season though, that she'd informed Layla and I that she might have to close the farm.

That day in their kitchen, I'd tried to squelch the suspicions rising inside me at the sight of that gold-lined velvet pant leg with the white furry cuff, but doing so proved to be as impossible as untangling a string of Christmas lights. So, when Layla and Molly turned on a movie, I excused myself to go to the bathroom, then veered off to Molly's bedroom to investigate. To my confusion, the garment bag that hung on her door didn't contain the entire Santa suit. It just held Santa's pants. Imagine my surprise two days later, when I found out that another tree had been stolen, and that this time around the Evergreen Bandits had left Santa's pants behind on the tree's stump.

I didn't have to be Sherlock Holmes to figure out the rest.

Heck, even Scooby Doo and his gang of friends could unmask this bandit. Molly Shanahan had been staging tree robberies to create fake news about the farm, hoping that this would drum up business. Her idea to sensationalize the robberies by leaving pieces of Santa's costume behind was just the brilliant icing on the cake. Seriously, someone call the Hallmark channel because it turns out all those robberies were just about saving the farm.

The only problem with Molly's plan, was what would happen if she were found out. Sure the people of Superior Falls had enjoyed the excitement and intrigue of it all, but nobody liked finding out they'd been played the fool. More importantly, the police had been expending resources to help her solve this crime. I'd seen enough crime shows to know that wasting police officers' time was public mischief, an offense that could result in a hefty fine or possibly even jail time.

At first, I hadn't been worried about her getting caught. After all, at that point there were only two days until Christmas. It seemed like she was on her way to getting away with the whole thing. Plus, with the secret celebrity she had coming, it looked like she would also actually end up saving the farm. And not because of my free elf labor.

But then that evening, as I was leaving my shift at Christmas Wonderland, I overheard Vince talking to one of the farm employees. A burly guy named Kirk, whose main job was helping families transport their trees correctly. Lots of people showed up with just a single bungee cord or, sometimes, nothing at all. Kirk, though this was only his second year on the farm, was excellent at upselling additional bungee cords, rope, and even blankets for people who didn't want to risk scratching the top of their cars. Vince was telling Kirk how he thought Sheriff Tom was going about this investigation all wrong.

"I mean how many Santa suits are lined with gold silk?" He asked Kirk. "But Tom thinks that's a negligible detail." Vince scoffed. "He just wants us to keep spending our evenings patrolling the place. Like I want to spend my Christmas Eve driving around here. We should've solved this case by now."

"Don't you have to work anyway?" Kirk asked. "What does it matter if you're driving around here or driving around somewhere else?" At this Vince rolled his eyes, then stalked off.

My heart almost stopped in my chest at Vince's words. Very few people outside of the Shanahan family knew about the gold silk that lined their famous Santa suit. Molly and Layla always called it their secret ingredient to a magical Christmas. Telling me had basically been their way of initiating me into the family. But if Vince was brandishing that tidbit of information around town, it still posed a risk. Especially if Layla heard it. What would she think of her mom's scheming? After graduating from Bay college last year, she'd taken this past year off, but in the spring, she planned on applying to law schools. Having a mom with a criminal record, would definitely not help her chances. I'd already experienced the downfall of my own dreams. I didn't want to watch my best friend go through the same thing. Not to mention the idea of Molly going to jail made me sick to my stomach. And now Vince had gone and told Kirk, who interacted with dozens of people each day as he loaded their trees, all about the gold-lined suit. The one thing that could get Molly caught.

I spent the next 24 hours trying to come up with some way to get them out of this. I made lists, researched *'excuses for robberies that will get you out of jail time'* on the internet, and stared vacantly into space awaiting inspiration. Finally, I resigned myself to the plan I'd tried to execute. Transfer the blame to myself. After all, Molly wouldn't press charges, and what did I really have to lose? My promising career as a learn-to-skate coach? Ha! I think I could recover. My parents' approval? I'd already lost that the minute the doctor said I could no longer figure skate competitively. Tarnishing my own reputation around town paled in comparison to Molly and Layla having theirs ruined.

Of course, now that I'm sitting across from the sheriff, the whole plan seems ridiculous. And the thought that Layla could've been involved the whole time, makes ice run down my spine.

"Cassie," Tom is peering at me kindly, "you look like you've just seen the ghost of Christmas past. Maybe you'd like a cup of cocoa before we continue?" He eyes his watch. "It's getting late, but hopefully Molly will arrive soon and help us get this sorted out. I know you two are close. She worries about you-" Abruptly he cuts himself off, his mustache twitching. He looks distinctly uncomfortable. My brain whirs.

"How do you know Molly worries about me?" I ask.

"What?" He blusters a bit. "Did I say that? I meant, I'm sure the idea that you would rob her would worry her." He stands suddenly, overturning his papers and knocking his chair down. "I think that's enough questions for now. I'll go get you that hot chocolate, then take you back to the holding cell."

He doesn't look at me as he gathers up the papers he's dropped, then practically sprints out the door. I stare after him. Trying to make sense of what just happened. Molly talks to Tom about me? Molly talks to Tom at all?

I put my arms on the table, then rest my head on them. Another mystery to solve. This time while I'm stuck inside a police station with the former love of my life. And to think, usually I spend Christmas Eve at church.

CHAPTER EIGHT-SPENCER

To the parent/guardian of Spencer Owens:
You are receiving this letter to notify you of your student's suspension from school due to his violation of the school's code of conduct. He may return to school on February 26.
   Sincerely,
   Principal Otis Mack
   Lake Superior High

Genevieve, on a personal note, I must implore you to try and keep Spencer in line. My staff and I are quite aware of the students' affinity for this Dare Wars game, and while much of it is innocent fun, this recent dare has crossed a line. I cannot have my students defacing school property-even if it is, as he claimed, in the name of supporting one of our students at her upcoming figure skating competition.
-Otis

Otis,
Goodness, it's washable window marker and some pithy cheers. I'd hardly call what Spencer did defacing school property. Still, I've sent him to the school to wash off his doodles. No harm, no foul, as I see it.
-Genevieve

The cell feels so much worse without Cassie in it. Almost immediately I go back to imagining ways to escape out of this place. This time thinking back to *The Count of Monte Cristo*. He got out of prison at the end of that book, right? I can't remember clearly, since I never actually made it through the book. Did he fake his own death? Or was it the guy from the Harry Potter books who did that? Not important. What I should really be thinking about right now, is how I can make Cassie understand why I left.

My mind plays back over the years of our relationship. I'm pretty dang sure I fell in love with Cassie the day she dared me to go out on the ice in my boxers and a T-shirt. Sure, I was only seven, but some girls just fit you right.

Sadly (and pathetically), it wasn't until the summer before high school that I finally got the courage to make a move. Even though she was a figure skater and I was a hockey player, our practice schedules overlapped. Since the rink was thirty minutes away, her parents and my grandma carpooled to get us to and from the rink each morning and evening. We went straight from morning practices to school where our schedules often perfectly aligned thanks to our tiny school. Evening practices often blurred into dinners together or late-night study sessions. Basically, the only time we weren't together was when we were on the ice or sleeping. I could not get enough of her.

Then summer came and threatened to take her away from me. She was going to an elite skating camp for six weeks. I was headed to a USA hockey camp for a month.

The day before we were both going to ship out, we were hanging out at the rink for open skate. As usual, Cassie wanted to be in the middle of the ice practicing her spins and jumps, rather than just skating around the rink like the casual skaters. Since I only wanted to be where she was, I hung out in the middle too, trying not to be obvious about watching her glide along the ice. I don't think it was just the hockey player in me that found her skating prowess hot.

"Why aren't you skating more?" Cassie asked me after having just landed a double axel.

"Just thinking about the summer." I tried to sound nonchalant and not like I'd just had to surreptitiously wipe some drool off my chin. "I think this is the longest we've ever been apart, you know, not counting the first four years of our life."

"I know." Cassie sobered a little. "Who am I going to dare for the next six weeks?" She put her finger to her chin in contemplation. "I'll have to find someone at camp. Maybe whoever they partner me up with will be up for some fun."

I was about to laugh, when her words sank in. "Wait, you're going to have a partner?"

"Yeah, didn't I tell you that? We get to work on both a solo routine and a pairs routine. I'm excited. I've never really had a skating partner before."

"A skating partner. What like a guy?" My mouth felt dry.

"Of course, silly." Cassie shoved my hip lightly with hers, sending sparks through my body.

"Oh." Jealousy clawed through me like a lion baring down on its prey. Cassie was going to be spending the next six weeks with another guy. A guy who would get to hold her hand, smell her vanilla scent, touch her body in the name of their stupid routine, see her in her skating skirts. The ones that showed so much leg I had a hard time focusing on her face when she wore them. (Don't think less of me-I was 14 and full of hormones I didn't know what to do with.)

"You okay, Spence?" Cassie skated backwards, lifting her arms gracefully over her head.

An idea formed in my head. "Fine. Just thinking, are you nervous about having a partner for the first time? Maybe you need to practice." I skated towards her, holding out my hand to her. "What do you say Cassie Chassé?" I tried to sound casual, and prayed she didn't see how badly my hand was shaking. How was it possible for my palms to sweat on an ice rink?

"You want to partner skate?" She eyed me dubiously. "You don't even have a toe pick." Her lips curved up in a mischievous smile, and I knew then that she was going to say yes.

"I'll make do." I tapped the ice with the curve of my blade, then met her gaze. "I dare you to give it a try." Channeling the moves I'd only ever seen in the made for TV Hallmark movies Cassie sometimes made me watch, I skated closer till we were less than a foot apart. "Or are you scared?" I whispered, looking down at her. Her eyelashes fluttered, and I almost lost my footing, ruining the romance, but then she took my hand, and I stayed standing.

Perfect. That was the word that settled in my chest as her hand slid into mine.

"Let's skate," my voice cracked embarrassingly, but Cassie didn't comment. Just nodded.

"Follow my lead, hockey boy." She glided forward, and I hurried to keep up. Figure skating is different than hockey skating, the blades of the hockey skate designed for speed and power while figure skates have longer blades with toe picks to help with balance. Cassie glided effortlessly around the ice, her body moving in time to the music played by the rink. Desperate to prove to her that I could be the partner she wanted, I adjusted my usual skating gait to something smoother. Then, because I'd seen enough skating routines to know what some of the moves looked like, I took a leap of faith and pulled her into a spin. A slow dance atop the icy surface. By some miracle I stayed standing as she gasped in surprise. My heart rate accelerated when she relaxed into me.

"Spencer Owens," she whispered up at me, "who knew you were

hiding a figure skater underneath all that hockey gear?"

I laughed. "You like that, huh?" Cassie's answering blush made me even bolder. "I've got another dare for you then."

"Oh?"

"I dare you to k-" the words died on my lips, as uncertainty came roaring back. What if she said no, and our whole friendship was ruined? My hesitation didn't matter though, because a second later she kissed me anyway. And that was that. She was mine, and I was hers. We both went to our respective camps, but at the end of every day we snuck away to spend the evening hours on the phone with each other. Late at night, as I laid in bed trying to fall asleep, I'd think about her kiss and how much I couldn't wait to be with her again. Funny how, when I left five years ago, I slipped back into that same habit. Each night, falling asleep to her face, wondering if somewhere she was missing me too. Wondering if I'd ever be able to hold her again.

I can't just sit here anymore. I stand up and start pacing the cell. My eyes land on something white in the corner. My heart rate accelerates as I reach down to pick it up and realize what I'm holding. It's a piece of Cassie's list. It must have fluttered in here when she tore it up.

Eagerly I read it. *9. Who knows what kind of women he's been dating while in New York. He probably doesn't even know how to kiss a regular woman anymore.* I shake my head as I read this. If only she knew what a hermit I've been. How for me Cassie has never been just a regular woman. She's always been the only woman.

10. He left. Nausea sweeps over me as I read this one. It doesn't make sense. She wanted me to go. Didn't she? I left because I thought Cassie hated me for what happened. I thought getting the heck out of her life was what she wanted. But after today, I'm not so sure.

My eyes slide down to the last item. It's written in glittery red ink instead of the blue pen the other items were transcribed in. She was using a red pen to write down customers' names and their corresponding photo orders at the farm today. This reason to stay away from me must have been a late addition, written after she'd already seen me again. The words spark hope inside me, and for the first time in five years my smile doesn't feel forced. *11. I think I still love him…how pathetic is that?*

CHAPTER NINE -CASSIE

Flatlander: what residents of the Upper Peninsula call visitors from the Lower Peninsula

Rather than returning with it himself, Tom sends Vince in with my hot chocolate. His cheek is still red from where I slapped him, and the sour look on his face lets me know he's still mad as heck at me. Still, the fact that Tom sent him in here must mean Vince hasn't mentioned it to him. If Tom knew that Vince was as irritated with me as a hungry flatlander who just realized the local grocery store isn't open on Sundays, I don't think he would've sent him in to get me. He seems too noble for that kind of behavior.

"Your hot chocolate." Vince sets the Styrofoam cup down so hard, liquid splashes over the top. "Tom said you could drink it in here, but after you assaulted me earlier, I think it'd be wiser to get you back in that cell as soon as possible." He glares at me, crossing his arms over his chest. "C'mon, up, up," he commands when I don't move.

"Did Tom have you patrol the farm every night?" I ask instead of doing as he says.

"What?" Whether he's taken aback by the question itself or the fact that I'm asking him questions instead of listening to him, I'm not sure.

"Did Tom have you patrol the farm every night?" I repeat slowly. "Or did he do it some nights as well?" I add.

Vince frowns. "I'm the cop here, Cassie. I'm the one who gets to ask questions."

"Right." I lean back against my chair, trying to look casual and unconcerned as I figure out how to play this. Vince loves to complain. So, if I can just get him going about how much abuse he suffers under Tom's reign, he'll likely give me the information I need. "Sorry, I was just wondering because you were the one who picked Spencer and I up. You're the one I always see hanging around the farm doing important investigative work. Doesn't seem like Tom has much of a hand in things." I look up at him with my best big innocent doe eyes. "Maybe you should be sheriff."

Vince narrows his eyes at me, and for a second, I think I've taken things too far. Surely, he'll see through my grandiose flattery. I just slapped this man thirty minutes ago. But then he clicks his tongue. "Believe me, you're preaching to the choir, Cassie. Tom's going about this whole investigation all wrong. I mean, sure, he's been out there patrolling the farm too. Or at least he says he has. But if he's actually patrolling the place, then how come the last three robberies all took place on his watch? Personally, I think Tom's got a new girlfriend, and he's bringing her on the stakeouts and getting distracted." He aims a wicked grin at me. "I know I wouldn't mind having some company on patrol nights." His grin vanishes. "Not you though. At least not anymore. I prefer my dates to be of the non-violent variety."

I barely hear him. He thinks Tom has a new girlfriend? And all the robberies have taken place on the nights Tom has been patrolling? Does that mean...Is it possible that Molly and Tom are *dating*?

"Have you seen her?" I forget about trying to flatter him as the question flies out of mouth.

"Who? The woman I'm replacing you with? I've got a few candidates in mind." He shrugs. "I heard Jessica Andrews is single again."

I bite my lip, trying to stay patient. "I heard that too. But I actually meant Tom's new girlfriend. Have you seen her?"

Vince grunts in annoyance.

"You know," I quickly add, "Jessica's niece is in my Thursday learn to skate class. When her sister has to work late, Jessica often brings her." I toss my hair. "I'd be happy to put in a good word for you with her. Tell her how good you look in uniform." Wow, I am really bringing it. I feel like some sort of secret agent or maybe a Bond girl. Do the Bond girls actually help James Bond though? Or are they just there for show? Not relevant. I refocus my thoughts on Vince, batting my eyelashes for good measure.

"I do look good in my uniform." Vince nods, sticking his thumbs through the belt loops of his pants and puffing out his chest. I force an admiring gaze his way. Vince preens.

"Of course," I go on, "when you start dating Jessica you won't be as careless as Tom. You'd never let yourself get distracted on the job."

"I don't ever get distracted when I'm on the job," Vince declares proudly. "I'm the one who nabbed you and Owens aren't I? Like I said, Tom's been too busy with his new girlfriend to focus."

"Not easy to distract *and* observant." I nod approvingly. "You don't miss a thing around here, do you?"

"Nope."

"Does that mean you know who Tom's new girlfriend is?"

"Nah." Vince shakes his head. "I've only ever seen the back of her head. He's been dang secretive about the whole relationship. But I can tell you with certainty that she was in the car with him the night of the last robbery. I found her hair on the seat of the patrol car the next day. Long and brown, so could be anyone really."

I fight to keep my expression neutral. He's right. Lots of women in Superior Falls have long, brown hair. But Molly is one of those women. And somehow, I don't think that's a coincidence.

"Enough chit-chat though." Vince goes back to the door. "Let's get you back to the cell."

CHAPTER TEN-SPENCER

Dear Spencer,

I've been thinking about this whole us going our separate ways in August business, and I've decided I hate the idea. I'm thinking maybe I go to Ann Arbor with you instead of doing the whole figure skating competition circuit thing. I mean, I don't want to be the pathetic girlfriend who follows her boyfriend to college, but I also really want to follow you to college. So where does that leave me?

Here's a secret I haven't told you. I used some of my babysitting money to apply to Concordia. It's a small private college down there. And guess what? I got in! I was thinking I might major in business. I have this idea to open my own skating academy. I know, it's crazy, but a girl can dream. I love figure skating, but lately some of the joy has gone out of it. It's always about the next competition, and how can I get better, be better. The thing is, I think I'm the best I'll ever be, and it's still not enough. But teaching little kids to skate- that sounds so joyful. My dad will never go for it, obviously. I'm not even sure why I bothered applying. And I'll never know what you think about the idea, since I absolutely will not actually be giving you this letter. If you're okay with us going our separate ways, I don't want to be the one whining about it. How depressing. Excuse me while I go drink my weight in hot chocolate. Just kidding. I would never do that.

Shh! Don't tell my dad I drink hot chocolate at your house, okay? That is so not part of a figure skater's diet.

Love,
    Cassie (that's right, love...again, you'll never get this letter, so I can be honest about my feelings for once.)

Even though I want nothing more than to talk to Cassie, I can't help the scowl that appears on my face when I see Vince escorting her back to our cell. I don't want that guy anywhere near her.

"Simmer down Owens," Vince doesn't miss my anger, "this isn't a hockey game. You can't just get put in the penalty box for a minute then hop back in the game. So, keep your rage in check." He grins, pleased with his reference.

"Just keep your hands off her," I growl as he sticks the key in the lock.

"What did you say?" Vince rubs his ear like he hasn't heard me, then turns and pulls Cassie into the cell by the elbow. "Nice chatting with you Cassie. If things don't work out with Jessica, maybe I will give you a call after all. I know I said I like non-violent women, but if dating you is going to make Owens this mad, I'm willing to give it a try. I'll even agree to drop the assault charges."

"Vince," Tom's voice spikes the air, halting my retort on my lips, "that's enough. This case is about to wrapped up. It's late. It's Christmas Eve. Go be with your family."

"You want me to go?" Vince looks put-out as he drops Cassie's elbow and faces Tom. "I'm the one who solved this case, Tom. I brought these robbers in! And now you just want me to go? What, so you can take the credit?"

"Officer Pacini," there's a note of warning in Tom's voice now, reminding me of the time in high school that he caught me in the grocery store parking lot installing bright pink rims to Vince's truck (another Cassie dare), "I think you should stop talking now. I really don't want to have to put you on probation for insubordination or, frankly, for your unprofessional behavior towards Cassie and Spencer."

"Me? Unprofessional?" Vince sputters. "She hit me!" He points indignantly to Cassie, reminding me of a child tattle-tailing on their sibling. "That's assaulting an officer!"

Next to me Cassie sucks in a breath. I can feel the tension emanating from her. "Only because you were making inappropriate advances on her," I interject quickly. "You deserved that slap." I fight the urge to pull Cassie against myself, wanting to give her strength in this moment. But we really need to talk before I do anything physical like that.

"We'll see what a judge thinks," Vince retorts.

"Enough!" Tom shouts. "Office Pacini, you are on dangerous ground. After what I've seen from you tonight, if you wanted to press charges against Cassie, I'd be in court testifying in her favor. So, I highly suggest you reconsider." He looks down at his watch. "It's 9:45. Why don't you go on to your sister's house. I heard you mention earlier to Officer Kropki that she was hosting a gathering that you were," he coughs and raises a pointed eyebrow, making it clear he's editing the actual words Vince said, "*unhappy* to miss. Enjoy Christmas with your family. And I expect that if you want to return to work on the 26, you'll come with a new attitude."

Vince's hands are balled into fists at his sides, but he doesn't say anything else. Just shoots me a death stare, then marches off, slamming the door behind him. Cassie exhales a long shuddery breath. I can't fight off the need to support her any longer. My hand seems to move of its own volition, finding hers and giving it a reassuring squeeze. Hope expands in my chest when she responds by interlacing her fingers with mine and squeezing back. It's the briefest of moments before her hand retreats back to her side, but I hold unto that moment, letting it start to erase some of the loneliness of the last five years.

"Alright then," Tom clears his throat, "back to business. You two will be glad to know that Molly Shanahan has arrived. She assured me she won't be pressing charges and is filling out paperwork for your release right now. Your grandma is here as well, Spencer. I guess Ms. Shanahan called her." He looks uncomfortable suddenly. "And, uh, there's someone else here too." His eyes flit to Cassie. "I'm not sure how they found out you were here…that's a small town for you, I suppose. Molly, I mean, uh, Ms. Shanahan is trying to get them to calm down."

I eye Cassie in confusion. What is Tom talking about? Who's here? Cassie doesn't look back at me though, her eyes are darting around the cell as if looking for a last-minute escape, and she's chewing her lower lip in a way I find very distracting. I don't have to ask who Tom is talking about though, because a second later they come bursting through the door. George and Helen Whitley. Cassie's parents. I barely notice her mom though, my gaze goes straight to her father. The man who, five years ago, stood outside Cassie's hospital room, and told me Cassie didn't want to see me. Who told me she wanted me to leave and never come back.

CHAPTER ELEVEN-CASSIE

Cassie Chassé-Can't believe we both leave tomorrow. One last dare before we go? I dare you to meet me at midnight outside your house. I managed to get my hands on a set of keys to the rink, and I want to have one last skate with you before I go. Make sure that when you're skating with that Jasper King character, you remember how much hotter it was skating with me.

-Spence

Spencer- I'll see you tonight.
♡
-Cassie

P.S. Hey, if you want to drop the hockey stick and take up figure skating, I'd take you as my partner in a second.

August 2018-The Night of the Accident

At five to midnight, I quietly open my window, then shimmy myself unto the ledge, before letting myself fall to the ground. Spencer's wide grin is the first thing I see as I land lightly on by back lawn.

"I'm going to miss seeing you jumping from that window," he says as he pulls me into him for a kiss. His words rub salt on the gaping wound that's been stretching itself across my heart every time I think about us going our separate ways.

Spencer leaves for the University of Michigan tomorrow. Never one who loved school, he decided to accept their hockey scholarship in the hopes that he'll get drafted after only a year or two of playing there.

As for me, tomorrow I head to Philadelphia for the Philadelphia Summer International. I've been going to national competitions pretty regularly for the past four years, but now that I've graduated high school, my parents hope to make it my full-time career. My last performance in New York caught the attention of a male skater named Jasper King. King has medaled at the last three World Championships, and his coach told mine that if I place at the Philadelphia Summer International, Jasper is interested in becoming my partner for pairs skating this season. So, no pressure or anything. Of course, if he does decide he wants me as his partner, I'll have to relocate to Denver, Colorado, where King currently lives and trains. My dad is beyond excited about the whole thing, but I'm just trying to ignore the growing feeling that I can't do this. I'm not cut out for it. As for when I'll see Spencer next, I have no idea. Not that he and I have talked about it. We've both been staunchly avoiding the topic of our separation.

I shake these melancholy thoughts away as Spencer pulls away and slips my hand into his. "You ready for this, Cass?"

"Ready." I nod, only able to manage that one word thanks to the lump that's formed in my throat. Spencer leads me quietly across the lawn and over to his truck, parked three houses down. We drive most of the way to the ice rink in silence, our hands still linked, resting on the center console, the quiet sounds of country music playing on his truck radio.

The parking lot of the rink is predictably empty. Spencer selects a spot behind the rink, hiding his car in the shadows of the dumpster, then runs over to my side of the truck to open my door.

"How did you manage to get a key again?" I ask, hoping to distract myself from the sadness sitting on my chest.

"I'm not sure I should give away my secret," Spencer gives me a wink as he slides the key into the lock. "I'd prefer for you to head off tomorrow with your head full of memories of my awesome prowess and mysterious ways."

I force a laugh, praying it doesn't turn into a sob. I'm grateful for the darkness of the lobby. It gives me a second to get ahold of myself. Spencer offers me his hand again.

"I don't want to turn on any lights in here," he tells me. "So, just follow me." Both of us have been to this arena so many times, we have no trouble navigating our way to one of the rinks. Once inside, Spencer locates the light switch and flicks it on. I blink rapidly as light fills the space. At first, I don't see what he's done, but then my eyes adjust and land on the picnic blanket spread out in the middle of the ice. A basket and two oversized pillows to use as seats are on top of the blanket.

"Spencer," my hands fly to my mouth as I turn to him, unable to keep my tears at bay anymore. "You did this, for me?"

Spencer immediately looks embarrassed, and I find this so adorable that I drop my skating bag to the floor, throw my arms around him, and starting kissing him over and over. Spencer laughs, then hoists me up so that our heads are level before taking control of the kiss, slowing it down so that every sensation rocks through my body. I want to stay in this moment forever.

When the kiss finally ends, he looks down at me with so much tenderness, that I can't keep the words I've been holding back for so long from bursting out.

"Don't go Spencer!" I cry. "Or I won't go. Whichever. Just. Please. Stay with me." As soon as the words are out, I want to swallow them back up, because he's not looking at me with tenderness anymore. No, the only word to describe the look on his face is horror.

"I'm sorry," I quickly retreat, "that was ridiculous. I didn't mean it. I just..." I trail off, desperate to erase my pathetic breakdown from history, "Should we just skate?" I bend down to retrieve my bag.

"Cassie," Spencer begins, but I don't look at him, I just keep rummaging through my bag, blinded by the tears swimming in my eyes. "Cassie," he repeats more loudly, tugging on my elbow.

I take a deep breath, mentally running through my skating routine for the competition next week in an attempt to dry up my tears. "Spencer," I finally look at him, giving him a big smile, "forget it. Let's skate." I pull away from him and march over to the bench, yanking my skates out of my bag as I go. Spencer is quiet for a few beats, but then heads over and sits next to me. Silently we put our skates on, but then as I rise to go onto the ice, he tugs my elbow once more.

"Wait, Cassie. C'mon. Were you serious?" I can't read the tone of his voice. My own emotions are too distracting.

"Spencer," I say in my best no-nonsense voice, "I said, let's skate." I pull my arm free and practically sprint to the rink, letting the familiarity of the solid ice beneath my blades calm my nerves. Only a few seconds go by before I feel Spencer come up behind me.

"Cassie, will you just hold on for one second?" He still wants to talk about it. I cringe. I don't want to hear him let me down gently. I should never have said anything. I just need to distract him.

"Spencer," I turn to face him, skating backwards along the ice, "you got one last dare in, so I think it's only fair that I get one too."

"What?" He looks confused. "Cassie, no. I don't want to do a dare. I want to talk about-"

"Remember back when we were freshmen," I cut him off, "and you tried to do some figure skating moves with me, because you were jealous that I was going to be skating with some random guy at skating camp?"

Spencer nods. "Yes, of course I remember. That was the day of our first kiss."

"Yeah," I offer him a brief smile, "it was."

"Cassie," Spencer speeds up, skating towards me. Gosh, he's being persistent. Let my embarrassment die in peace, I want to shout, no need to revive it. I've signed it's DNR paperwork-DO NOT RESUSCITATE!

"You want to recreate that moment," I ask, trying to sound flirtatious.

"No, I want to talk," Spencer stops skating. He's right next to the picnic blanket he set up, and he gestures to it. "So why don't you come sit down."

I shake my head. "I want to skate with you. After next week, I'll probably be skating with Jasper King all the time, and you promised me that tonight you'd make sure I remember you when I'm skating with him. Are you not up to the challenge?" I stare him down, then lay my trump card. "I dare you to skate with me, Spencer Owens. Make me forget all about Jasper King."

He'd been about to push back, but my name dies on his lips at these last few words. "Fine. Come here." His voice is husky and commanding. A shiver of pleasure runs down my spine, and I bite back a smile as I glide towards him. He catches me by the waist, then spins me around so that my back is to his chest. "Tell me what to do first." His voice is low, his lips right next to my ear. I feel my breathing quicken.

"First," I say shakily, "we stare into each other's eyes." I look up at him, committing the exact shade of his green eyes to memory before moving on to the next step. "Then, in theory, the music would start, and we'd set off in unison." I push off from him, and he mimics my movements. We skate backwards along the ice, his hand fluttering only inches from mine. I spin back to face him, offering him my hand. "Now, pull me into your body, then lift me gracefully into the air."

Spencer does as I say, taking my hand in his giant one and tugging me towards himself. He lifts me carefully into the air, wobbling only slightly before lowering me back to the ice. "Not bad, hockey boy," I say. I can feel a familiar edge of recklessness creeping in. It's the same recklessness that's kept me performing and divvying out dares all of these years. It's the recklessness that comes from being afraid of failing everybody around me. "But you know, all the best figure skating routines have jumps. Do you hockey players do that? Or do I need to teach you?" I don't wait for an answer, instead I glide away, gaining speed before leaping up into a double axel.

I land smoothly, then head back towards him. He's shaking his head ruefully at me. "Maybe I should just grab my hockey stick, and I can teach you how to shoot."

"Spencer," I chastise, "are you trying to get out of a dare? How about I take it easy on you? You don't have to do any actual jumps, you can just catch me after I jump."

"That sounds slightly more doable," he concedes, though he still looks doubtful.

"Okay then." I grab his hand again. "First, we have to skate together, then you lift me up and push me high enough into the air that I can get at least a double rotation before coming back down for you to catch."

"What? Cassie, no." He shakes his head. "I'm not trained for that. You could get hurt."

"Please. With figure skating there's always a risk of getting hurt. I fall all the time. You get back up and move on. It's part of learning. Don't ruin the moment, Spencer. This is our last skate together for a long time." I don't know why I'm pushing this. I feel desperation rising inside me, like I just want to be free of something. Only I don't know what exactly I'm seeking freedom from. My dad's expectations? My obligation to compete? Any future where I don't see Spencer every day?

"Yeah, I guess." Spencer shrugs. "But you have a competition in a few days, why risk an injury?"

"There's no risk," I lie. "I'm sure you'll catch me." Without waiting for him to protest further, I start skating, my forward movement propelling him by our linked hands.

"Cassie," he tries to tug me back, but I pull out of his grasp, annoyed.

"Fine Spencer, we'll do things your way," I call to him as I skate away. "*Dirty Dancing* style, catch and lift." I don't wait for a reply, just start skating fast towards him. I know he'll get the reference. I've made him watch that movie, that scene dozens of times over the years, completely in love with Johnny and Baby's story. Sure enough, when he sees me coming fast at him, he bends his knees, readying to catch me despite the wide-eyed horror on his face.

"Cassie no!" he starts to say, but it's too late, I'm already leaping into the air. A second later his hands are on my waist lifting me up, and it's fine. We've done it. I smile broadly. But then suddenly I'm falling. As I look down, I see his skate tangled in the picnic blanket, throwing off his balance. I crash to the ground, trying to catch myself on my leg, but my ankle twists painfully, my head smacks the ice, and everything goes black.

CHAPTER TWELVE-CASSIE

To choke (sports): to fall short of expectations in a competition or game

"Cassie! Oh Mylanta! George, our baby is in jail!" My mother's voice ricochets off the walls in its hysteria as she and my dad burst into the room.

"Yes, I can see that, Helen." My dad's baritone voice holds even more than its usual notes of displeasure. "And look who put her there."

"Spencer! Spencer Owens!" Her exclamation is somewhere between thrilled and angry. How my mother manages to convey such a vast array of emotions with just her tone is beyond me.

"Heard you were back in town," my dad grunts. "One of your grandma's harebrained schemes to save the tree farm. Far as I know she's never even bought a tree there, now suddenly she's championing the place." Another grunt. "Humph. Seems like all she's done is mess up my daughter's life again." He crosses his arms across his chest, staring Spencer down.

"Oh George," my mom frets, "you know Genevieve was just trying to help out Molly. I'm sure she didn't intend for her grandson to get our daughter arrested when she asked him to come home."

"Harumph," is all my dad says to this.

"Dad stop." I can't take this anymore. Ever since the accident my dad, who used to love Spencer, has been bent on telling anyone and everyone who will listen how Spencer ruined my life and doesn't deserve the success he's found with the New York Huskies. And I, ever the coward, have just stood silently by and let him say it. But I can't lie anymore. Not after tonight. "Spencer didn't get me arrested, dad. I got him arrested."

"What?" My dad's face whips to me. "What did you say?"

"Don't be silly dear." My mom approaches the bars holding her hands out in supplication like I'm a queen, and she'd like me to grant her humble request. "I'm sure that's not true. This is just another one of Spencer's little dares gone wrong. He always had a way of making you do things against your better judgment. Probably those eyes of his. So handsome." She sighs as she looks him up and down. "Would've made such gorgeous grandbabies the pair of you, if things had gone differently."

"Mom." I grip the bars. "Stop. Please. I'm not just a silly little girl who got herself caught up in the shady schemes of her boyfriend. I have always shared equal blame for the stunts Spencer and I pulled. You two just never wanted to see the truth." My voice cracks at conveying this long-withheld truth, and tears start to form in the corner of my eyes. "You just thought it was easier to blame him. You even enjoyed laughing at all of our antics, because you could just say they were his. Say it was just a guy being a guy, and I was just along for the ride. But it was me too mom and dad." Tears are falling freely now, but my mom still doesn't seem to have caught on.

"What are you talking about honey?" She shakes her head at me. "You're not making any sense."

"Mom, Spencer and I both organized the Dare Wars."

"No. That can't possibly be true." She shakes her head even harder, stepping back from the cell. "Everyone in town knows it was Spencer."

"No, mom," I say sadly, "it was both of us. Actually most of the time the dares were *my* idea. I dared Joe Dennison to drive his car into the football field and leave it there, not Spencer. And I dared Jessica Andrews to take Principal Mack's wrestling trophy and hide it in the corn maze at the orchard." I sniff loudly, but then press on, "I dared Carter Bradshaw to paint all the lines in the school parking lot purple. And Karen O'Malley spray painted the rock outside the school with Spencer's name and jersey number because I dared her to." I take a shuddery breath. Their mouths are wide open, gaping at me. But I can't stop now. It's time to say it.

"And five years ago, at the ice rink I dared Spencer to catch me. He didn't want to do it," I'm sobbing so hard I'm not sure they can even make out all my words, "but I made him. So, all this time you've been blaming him for ruining my life by ending my figure skating career, but the truth is, I ruined my own future. *I wasted all the money and time you spent on me. I floundered it all away* with my reckless choice. Me! Not him. And it was all because I was scared! Scared I couldn't cut it. Scared of disappointing everyone. And most of all, scared that Spencer and I were going down two different paths, and I was going to lose him." I don't dare look at Spencer as this last confession bursts out of my mouth. My chest is heaving like I just speed skated around a rink.

My parents are both just staring at me, their eyes wide as saucers, their jaws slack. I feel hot all over under the scrutiny. Worse, I feel the intensity of Spencer's eyes on me, but I'm too scared to see what exactly his gaze contains. Reproach? Disgust? Pity? It's all bad.

"Well dear, it's about time you said that all out loud." The lilting voice of Genevieve Owens momentarily draws the attention away from me. She stands in the doorway, an approving look on her face.

"Genevieve," my mom's hand flies to her throat, "you knew about all of this?"

"Not all of it," Genevieve waves her hand dismissively, "but my grandson did tell me what actually happened the night of Cassie's accident." Her gaze shifts to my dad. "Then just last month he broke down and told me about not only the conversation you had with him leading up to the accident, but the one you had with him after it as well." She frowns at him. "Let's just say that was illuminating." My dad spoke with Spencer? He never told me that. Just that Spencer had left. "George, I never would have thought you capable of-"

"Enough!" My dad slashes his hand through the air. "I don't want to hear anymore. First my daughter gets arrested. Then I find out she's been lying to me for most of her life, running around playing ridiculous pranks on people, then letting me blame her boyfriend for instigating everything." His face is getting redder and redder, matching the rapidly growing pit inside my stomach. "Now she tells me she threw all my hard work away because she got a little nervous! That she just choked!" A vein ticks in his temple. It's like the pounding of a hammer, squelching me into a tiny insignificant speck. I always knew I had failed my dad, but that doesn't make this blatant confirmation of that hurt any less. I'm just another story of an athlete who balked under pressure. Nothing new. Nothing special.

Yet even as I let his words weigh me down, I feel an urgent need to know what Genevieve is talking about. A need I can't suppress.

"What is she talking about, dad?" My voice comes out quiet, timid. I'm not used to standing up to my dad. That's why it was so easy to just let Spencer take the blame, and yes often the credit, for our dares over the years. To just go along with everyone's assumption that what happened that night was Spencer's fault.

But tonight has changed something inside of me.

"I'm not a little girl anymore, dad." I try to force more confidence into my voice, but it still shakes. "I know that I've let you down. I know that I acted impulsively and cowardly that night. I should've talked to you about all of the pressure I was feeling. I should've talked to Spencer about how afraid I was of losing him. But dad, I was 18." Even as I say these words and see zero hint that they have had any impact on him, I feel a strange sense of release. All of this time I've been carrying the weight of having ruined not only my life, but my parents' lives. But as I stand here, dressed in this ridiculous elf costume, I feel that weight fall off of me. I made a mistake. I don't have to go on living the life of a martyr because of it. I don't have to be defined by my dad's disappointment any longer.

"I was 18," I repeat into the heavy silence.

"About time you realized that." This comes from Molly Shanahan, who has joined the fray and is beaming at me.

"Here, here." Genevieve nods approvingly. "Goodness, the things I did when I was 18. Well, I'm sure you know what the seventies were like. Groovy, baby." She sighs as if remembering, and I find, despite my tension, I have to bite back a giggle.

"Molly," my dad is curt, "While I'm sorry for the damage my daughter has done to your tree business, I don't see a need for you to weigh in on her other life choices. So if you're not pressing charges, I'd rather you left, quite honestly."

"George is that necessary," my mom says in feeble reproof.

"I don't suppose it's up to you whether I stay or go, George." Molly stares him down.

"I quite agree." Genevieve primly adjusts the strap of her purse. "Anyway, I'm sure Molly will want to stick around to see how this plays out. The two of us have worked so hard to get to this point." She frowns as she eyes Spencer and I in our cell. "Well, actually I don't think we ever thought it would get to this point," she gestures to us, "but I think we'll still get our desired outcome."

"Yes, I think so too, Genevieve." Molly nods. "Certainly parts of our plan seem to have gotten out of hand, but since I'm not pressing charges, no harm, no foul."

"Grandma, what's going on?" Spencer finally breaks his silence. I allow myself a tiny peak at him, but his face is unreadable, all his attention focused on Genevieve.

"They're the Evergreen Bandits," I announce when Genevieve doesn't reply. "Molly, I knew it was you, but Genevieve was in on it too?"

"What?" My mom, my dad, and Spencer all chime in unison.

"Oh, no!" Genevieve shakes her head. "Goodness me, no." She shudders. "I detest thievery." She eyes Molly. "Though I admit, I did know Molly was behind all the missing trees. Still, stealing from oneself is not quite the same as actually stealing."

"More like relocating," Molly agrees with a grin. "A bit of tree feng shui, if you will."

"Mom?" Layla enters the room, her eyes on Molly. "*You're* the Evergreen Bandit? How? Why?" She looks around and spots Tom lurking in the corner. "Oh my gosh, and now you're confessing in front of an officer of the law! You're going to be arrested for public mischief! I'm going to have a mother with a criminal record!" She moans. "I'm not getting into law school, am I? Why? Why would you do this?"

"Oh honey, calm down." Molly puts her arm around Layla, shushing her.

"I wouldn't worry about her getting arrested, Layla," I pipe up, "since Tom has been working with her this whole time."

Now everyone's heads turn to Tom, their collective gasp so loud it's almost comical. I feel like I'm starring in a soap opera.

"No police resources were wasted," Tom announces in response to all the attention, "Vince may disagree, but frankly the most criminal action this town gets is the occasional drunk driver or a punk kid playing pranks." His eyes flit to Spencer with a reproving raise of his eyebrows. "Vince had to work the nights I sent him to patrol the farm anyway. So either he could have hung out here at the station or driven around the farm. Tomayto-tomahto in terms of tax payers' money."

"Whatever." Layla dismisses this with a wave. "I still don't understand why you would help my mom steal Christmas trees from her own farm?"

"They were trying to drum up hype, Layla," I explain. "Create fake news around the farm to bring customers in."

"What? That's ridiculous mom!" Layla cries. "And you!" Layla switches her wrath to me. "You knew about this, and you didn't tell me?"

"I only found out yesterday," I try to placate her, "and I thought I could take care of it. Make sure your mom never got caught."

"That's why you really stole the tree? To take the heat off Molly?" Spencer's green eyes pierce me. "There was no underprivileged skating student who needed it?"

I flush. "I'm sorry I lied to you. You were never supposed to come with me." It's a lame apology. "I-I never meant to get you arrested."

Spencer doesn't say anything, and I feel dread seep through me. I've messed things up so badly.

"I-I meant what I said earlier," I press on. "I can talk to your coach about what happened. Tell him it was all my fault."

Spencer's lip twitches, like he's trying not to laugh. Does he find this *funny*?

"So grandma," he rotates to face her again, "tell me, if Molly was already saving the farm with her whole fake tree robbery scheme, why your demanding request that I come home to play Santa and save the farm?" He cocks his head. "The farm I didn't even know you cared about."

"I should think that would be obvious," she replies, "but perhaps you've taken one too many blows to your noggin out there on the ice to realize what's going on." Genevieve taps her own white-haired head. "After what you told me on the phone a few weeks ago about your conversations with Cassie's father, I knew I had to take action." She gestures to me. "This one's been moping around town since you left." She eyes me. "No offense dear. You make quite a pretty mope, but, really, it was extremely obvious to everyone that you never got over my grandson."

I flush, once again unable to look at Spencer. Extremely obvious to everyone? Really?

"But the good news for you, Cassie, is that my grandson never got over you either. He simply got tricked by your rather unfortunate father." She eyes my dad like he's a piece of gum on her shoe.

My dad. Right. I got so caught up in the whole 'who stole the trees from the tree farm' debacle, that I almost let my dad get away with not explaining what exactly he said to Spencer.

"I didn't trick anybody," my dad scowls. "I simply pointed out what I thought were obvious truths." He narrows his eyes at Genevieve. "You can't honestly tell me you would've been happy about Spencer staying home and missing out on the hockey career he's achieved just so he could be with Cassie." I wince at his words, but he either doesn't notice or doesn't care. "They were kids Genevieve, just because Spencer thought he was in love with Cassie didn't mean they should both throw their lives away. He wanted to follow Cassie around the figure skating circuit, Genevieve. With only a high school degree to his name! I said what needed to be said."

My breath catches in my throat, and my whole body feels cold. I turn to Spencer, suddenly not wanting to hear what else my dad has to say. I only want to hear from Spencer. "You wanted to follow me?" I whisper.

Spencer looks sheepish, and his voice shakes a little as he replies. "Maybe."

"And y-you loved me?" Even after dating for four years, we'd never actually exchanged the words. There'd been dozens, no hundreds of times I'd wanted to, but fear had always held me back. What if he didn't say it back? What if I scared him away? So, I held in the words. Daring only to pen them in letters I never sent him.

This time his voice doesn't waver. "Of course I did."

I close my eyes, sinking into the warmth of his words. He *loved* me. Then I register the past tense of the word and feel a burst of gloom. "Then why didn't you say anything when I asked you to stay that night? When I told you I would go with you?" I look pleadingly at him, desperate for some explanation. "You looked horrified at the very thought."

"Horrified?" Spencer shook his head. "No, Cassie. I was just scared. I'd just talked to your dad a few days before about wanting to stay with you, and he freaked out at me. He told me there was no way I was going with you on the competition circuit. He railed on and on about how no daughter of his was attaching herself to a man without a plan for his future. He said that if I wanted a chance with you, I'd get my hockey career going, so I could be a good provider." He flushes. "He also said there was no way he would let you go with me, that he'd worked too hard to get you to where you were to watch you throw it away for a guy." He shrugged. "And to tell you the truth Cassie, I didn't want you throw away your skating career for me. I wanted you to be able to live your dream."

I don't have to ask him why he didn't just tell me all of that then. He tried. He tried over and over that night, but I wouldn't listen. I just kept pushing him to skate with me, trying to cover over the gaffe I thought I'd made by asking him to stay...by telling him, I'd go with him. I was such an idiot.

"But," I step towards him, the bells on my elf shoes jangling, "why didn't you stay after the accident? I tore my Achilles tendon. The doctor said I'd never skate competitively again. My career was already over. Why didn't you ask me to go with you at that point?"

Spencer looks confused. "Because, Cassie-"

"Enough!" my dad bellows. He's finished his conversation with Genevieve, and is now looking at Spencer with murder in his eyes. "This conversation is over. It's Christmas Eve. If no charges are being pressed, I'd like to take my daughter home." He turns to my mom. "Helen, let's go. Tom, unlock this door."

He looks expectantly at both of them, but neither one moves.

CHAPTER THIRTEEN-SPENCER

C.W.+O.S.
4eva

**(Inscription etched into the old oak tree
at the center of town, circa 2017)**

"Tom," George repeats, stepping closer to him, "I said, let's unlock the door. Get Cassie out of here."

I don't listen to Tom's reply, I'm too eager to get out what I have to say. I step closer to Cassie, trying not to draw her dad's attention away from Tom. "Cassie," I catch her attention with the urgent timbre of my voice, and she immediately looks away from her dad and back at me.

"What did he say to you Spencer?" she asks with wide eyes.

My eyes dart over to George, but he's still reading Tom the riot act. Now is my moment. "Cassie," I say her name again, wishing I could reach out and take her hands, "your dad told me you wanted me to leave. That you never wanted to see me again."

Memories rush in as I stare at her now ashen face. My foot catching on that stupid blanket. The feel of Cassie slipping through my fingers, falling to the ground, her foot going one way, her leg the other. Pop! Her head slamming the ice. Bam! The overwhelming panic that clouded my vision and cut off my breath when she didn't come to right away. Her eyes fluttering blessedly open a few seconds later, hooded in confusion, but open.

Realizing I'd left my phone in the car and, not willing to leave her, carrying her carefully out to my car, where I turned the heat on full blast and covered her in my coat to try and suppress her shivers. Cursing our town's ridiculous version of 911 as the operator, a guy named Benny Coats, tried to make small talk with me about the last hockey game he'd watched me play in. Driving her to the hospital when Benny informed me that our town's lone ambulance was already out responding to a call about an elderly gentleman having a stroke.

The doctor at the hospital asking what happened as he examined her ankle and peered into her pupils. Me lying. "We were just practicing her routine for her figure skating competition next week. I tripped on the ice and dropped her." Cassie's wide eyes landing on me at this lie. Me trying to silently communicate that it was fine. If we told the truth, that it had been Cassie who'd insisted I catch her, her dad would never forgive her. I would protect her. I had always protected her, and I would always protect her. No matter the detriment to myself. I could take her father's cutting words and scathing looks. I could handle his shouting, his criticism, his belittling if it meant she didn't have to be on the receiving end of any of it.

I remember the doctor refusing to let me go with her as they wheeled her back for an x-ray of her ankle. Having to call Cassie's parents from my chair in the cold, white waiting room. Standing outside her recovery room the next morning after her surgery, never even having gone home, and being told by her dad that I couldn't see her. "She'll never skate competitively again Spencer," he'd growled at me. "All because of you. She never wants to see you again. She wants you to leave and never contact her again." So, I left. Cassie didn't want me anymore, so I had nothing to stay for.

"He told you that I wanted you to leave?" Cassie's small voice pulls me from my memories.

"Yes," I nod, then look away from her, not wanting to see her face as I expose all of my vulnerabilities here in a freaking jail cell. Clearly I've got the romantic ambience side of things nailed. "But Cassie, after everything that's happened tonight, I have to know... was it true what he said? Did you want me to leave?"

A beat of silence passes, then I feel Cassie's soft hand cup my jaw, tugging it back to face her. "November 15, 2018," she says.

"What?" I study her, trying not to let the feel of her hand on my jaw distract me from what she's saying.

"That's the day my doctor cleared me to drive after my surgery," she goes on. "It's also the day I hopped in my car and drove the seven hours it took to get to Ann Arbor."

"You came to Ann Arbor?" I gape at her. "But I never saw you."

"I know, but I saw you." Her face turns wistful. "You had a game that night. I watched you from the stands. You looked so right out there, doing the thing you loved most. So, I decided I didn't want to wreck that for you." She sets her shoulders. "As far as I knew, you'd left by choice anyway. Who was I to swoop in and see if maybe there was a chance you were as miserable without me as I was without you?" Her eyes meet mine, and I see the pain there. I want to pull her against me in a hug and tell her just how dang miserable I was without her, but she keeps talking, so I wait.

"So I left right after the game. I was going to at least leave you a note, you know just to wish you well, say I was proud of you, and all that, but then I saw her."

"Her?" I'm lost. "Her who?"

"Oh wow." A flash of irritation crosses her face. "Have there been that many women since me, Spencer, that you can't even remember which one I'm referring to?"

"Uh, not to mess with your list of reasons to stay away from me, but to tell you the truth, Cassie, I haven't been with any other women since I left."

"Don't lie, Spence." She drops her hand from my chin, and I immediately mourn the loss. "I saw you come out of the arena with a blonde girl. She threw her arms around you, and you hugged her. It looked...intimate."

"A blonde girl who hugged me after a game?" I wrack my brain.

"Do you mean Jackson's girlfriend?"

"I don't know." Cassie scrunches her nose. "As far as I could tell she was *your* girlfriend."

"Well the only girl that ever hugged me after a game was Jackson's girlfriend Zoey. Jackson was my roommate at Michigan. His girlfriend, now wife, is extremely effusive. Very touchy feely. She hugs everybody."

She studies me as if trying to decide whether or not I'm telling the truth. "Cassie, I swear I've never dated another woman," I put my hands up in a show of innocence.

"Really? I mean obviously it would be okay if you had..." She swallows, then seems to force the next words out, "We weren't together."

"Cassie," I take her hands, then, steadied by her nearness, I risk it, "you are it for me. You have always been it for me."

Her answering sigh floods my senses with longing. "Spencer Owens," she steps closer to me, "I-"

"Now look what you've done!" Cassie's dad roars, finally noticing the two of us have been talking while he's been busy berating Tom. Honestly, I sort of forgot about all of the other people in the room, but now that I've remembered them all, I see my grandma and Molly shooting us furtive glances from the corner of the room, big smiles on their faces. Layla stands a few feet away from them, her eyes darting back and forth between

Cassie and I like she can't quite figure out what to think. Cassie's mom is just standing in the middle of the room, wringing her hands, whether because of her husband or her daughter and I, I'm not really sure. "You locked them in a cell under false pretenses and now they're practically kissing," George yells.

"Ooh, scandalous," Layla mutters, earning a look of derision from George.

"Let Cassie out," he growls at Tom.

"Actually Tom," my grandma speaks up, "I agree with George on this one thing, it's about time you let these two out."

"Certainly." Tom pulls out his keys and heads towards the door.

"Thank you, Tom," Molly says as he swings the door open.

"Of course, Molly dear." He tosses her an affectionate smile. I hear Layla gasp.

"Oh right," Cassie pipes up as she walks through the cell door, "I knew I was forgetting something. Layla," she eyes her friend, "your mom is dating Tom."

"What?" Layla exclaims. Immediately she and Molly start talking at the same time, their high-pitched voices echoing around the room.

"Oh dear." My grandma shakes her head at them, though she looks amused. "You two better get out of here," she says to Cassie and I. "Here, take my truck, Spencer. There's a surprise for you in the front seat." She passes me her keys just as George closes in on us.

"Cassie," he levels her with a glare, "I think you and I have a lot to talk about. Come on home with your mother and I."

"Dad," she sets her shoulders, "I'm 23. I love you, and I'm sorry about everything, but I'm not going to your house right now." She steps back from him. "And honestly, you owe me an apology too." Without another word, she sweeps out of the room. I follow her without even looking at George. There's a part of me that would like to stay and give him a piece of mind about lying to me five years ago, but there's a bigger part of me that just wants to go be with Cassie. I've missed out on five years with her. I'm not missing out on another second.

CHAPTER FOURTEEN-CASSIE

Molly Shanahan's Spiked Hot Chocolate:
Mix one hot chocolate packet into 8 ounces of warm milk.
Then pour in 1 ounce of mocha liqueur and ½ ounce vanilla
vodka. Top with whipped cream and crushed candy canes.

I don't stop moving until we're standing next to Genevieve's gray truck. My legs are shaking from the confrontational words I just said to my dad, and my heart is racing from getting so close to confessing my feelings to Spencer. The combination has the same effect on my head as too much of Molly's spiked hot chocolate, and I have to lean against the car to steady myself.

"Cassie," Spencer's deep voice pulls my eyes to his, "you okay?"

I laugh. "I can't believe I just did that."

"You were great." He reaches over and sweeps my hair off my face, letting his fingers linger on my temple.

"So where were we then?" I ask breathily.

"I think I was about to kiss you," he replies, his eyes drifting down to my lips.

"Then what are you waiting for?" I stand on my tip-toes, placing one hand on his chest.

"Cassandra Whitley! We are not done talking about this." Once again, my dad's abrasive voice interrupts the moment. I look over to see him emerging from the building, his eyes scanning the lot for me.

"Quick," Spencer hits the unlock button on the keys, "get in." He pulls the door open and gives me a boost up into the truck and over the center console. He follows me in, then wastes no time starting the truck and getting us the holly berry out of there.

We drive in silence, Spencer navigating us down the familiar roads of our small town to a spot I know well. It's one of Superior Falls' many corn fields, but this one is special. We used to drive out here and look at the stars, stealing kisses and sharing laughter. As he puts the truck in park, he looks over at me, and the fire in his eyes sends a thrill through me.

"I think we're alone now." His voice is low and husky. I want to rip that Santa suit right off him. I mean, he's wearing a t-shirt underneath, so it would totally be appropriate. Just less of a holly jolly type make-out session and more of a normal one.

"I think you're right," I reply like the verbal genius I am.

"Did I mention I missed you like crazy these last five years?"

"Did I mention I love you?" I say the words fast, not wanting to lose my nerve. Spencer's face breaks into a broad grin.

"Did I mention I love you too?" He leans across the center console to finally kiss me. His movement jostles the seat and something falls into the cupholder. We both look at the clump of evergreen leaves between us.

"Mistletoe?" I say in wonder.

"There's a note attached," Spencer pulls the small white card off the ribboned stem. "This must be the gift my grandma was talking about," he says in amusement as he opens the note.

"Wow, she really wants us to kiss," I say with a giggle as I lean over to read the note with him.

"Me and her both," Spencer says with a grin, "Seriously, when are all of these interruptions going to end?"

I grin back, then we both glance down at her note.

My darling Spencer and sweet Cassie,

If you're reading this note together, then my evil plan worked! Of course, no plan is complete without a dramatic ending. So, given the nature of your relationship growing up, I leave you this evergreen gift. Mistletoe-nature's very own dare to kiss the girl. So, there you go Spencer, kiss the girl-I dare you.

Love,
Grandma

As we both finish reading our eyes meet, and I swear the stars flicker from the electricity between us.

"Well," Spencer inches closer, "I never could say no to a dare." Then his lips are on mine, and my whole world tilts off its axis. No, scratch that, my whole world tilts back to where it was meant to be all along, right here next to Spencer. Turns out, he's not the only one who came home for Christmas.

EPILOGUE- CASSIE

Six Months Later

**Wall-Hugger: term used by experienced
skaters to refer to individuals
who need to stay by the wall in order to not fall on the ice**

"What do you think?" I spin around the small space, unable to keep the smile off my face.

"It's amazing Cass." Spencer looks around my new office, then gives a low whistle as his eyes land on a photo of me doing a double axel on the wall. "Who's the hot figure skater in this picture? I'd like to get to know her."

I laugh and slug him on the shoulder.

I moved down to New York a month after Christmas and quickly got myself a job teaching skating at a suburban ice rink. Somewhere along the way I told Spencer about my dream of opening up my own skating academy, and he encouraged me to set up meetings with some owners of local ice rinks about the possibility. And, miraculously, I found a rink that said yes! So now, I'm running The Evergreen Skating Academy at the Ice Station, a rink twenty minutes outside of Manhattan.

And the best part is, the money I've been saving up the last five years covers both my rent at the crappy apartment I found and at least my first few months of operating costs. I'm Miss Independent over here. Of course, if I don't manage to earn any revenue these next few months my independence might die, but Spencer is confident this won't be the case. And also more than willing to make me a small business loan that I can pay back in kisses. His suggestion, not mine. Though I did inform him he's not allowed to just give me money, like he keeps trying to do. I'll figure something out.

"Tell me," Spencer draws me closer to him with a tug on my hands, "what does a guy have to do to get a kiss from the owner of the Evergreen Skating Academy?"

"Hmm." I pretend to think. "Usually she only kisses guys dressed as Santa Claus, but I may be able to convince her to make an exception this time, you know, for a regular old hockey player like yourself."

Spencer laughs. He starts to bend down to kiss me, but then changes his mind and scoops me up instead, lifting me up in the air so that I'm looking down at him. "Have I ever told you," he asks, "how glad I am that you never partnered up with that Jasper King character?"

I laugh. "You're the only partner for me, Spencer Owens." He grins and spins me around, before lowering me so that our faces are level.

"I got you a present," he tells me.

"Oh? I hope it's not an envelope full of cash."

"Oh, don't worry, I don't need to give you an envelope of cash, since I already added your name to my bank account."

"Spencer!" I chastise, but he just laughs again, then sets me down.

"Here." He retrieves his hockey bag from where he deposited in the doorway when he arrived and, after unzipping it, pulls out a garment bag.

"What is this?" I ask in bewilderment.

"Open it."

I slowly unzip the bag, even more puzzled when I see a familiar shade of green fabric. "Oh my goodness! Spencer, is this what I think it is?"

"When I said I got you a present," Spencer replies airily, "I actually meant I got Molly a present."

I laugh as I pull out the elf costume.

"The truth is," he goes on, "I ordered this on Amazon the day after Christmas, but it only just arrived in Superior Falls last week. I had to have my grandma send it here."

"You're joking."

Spencer chuckles. "Yes, I just ordered this last week. I shouldn't make fun of our hometown though, not when I'm hoping you'll agree to go back there next Christmas to be the elf to my Santa once more."

"You really want to go back to the scene of our crime?" I ask, raising a playful eyebrow.

Spencer drops a quick kiss on my lips. "Seems like the perfect spot for a wedding, don't you think?"

"A wedding?" I eye him in confusion. "Who's getting married?" Even as I say the words, he drops to one knee.

"Cassie, I have loved you since we were just a pair of wall-hugging kids, and I know I'll love you until we're a pair of old timers who need to use walkers out there on the ice." He looks up at me, and one corner of his mouth slides up in a grin. "Now a normal guy would ask you to marry him, but nothing about the two of us is normal, so Cassie Chassé I'm not going to ask." He pulls a ring box from his back pocket and opens it. "Cassie Whitley, I dare you to marry me."

I laugh through the tears shimmering in my eyes.

"What do you say?" Spencer adds nervously, when I'm still laughing a few seconds later.

"Of course, I'll marry you," I beam. "I never say no to a dare."

ABOUT THE AUTHOR

 As a child, Heather Miekstyn used to spend hours in her room creating characters, then excitedly writing out the first half of their stories before inevitably losing steam. Then she discovered the romance genre and realized the key to finishing any good story-a happy ending. And also, lots of kissing. Heather resides in Michigan with her husband, four daughters, and their rambunctious black lab. When she is not writing, she can be found reading, running, or playing Bananagrams. She hopes her books leave you feeling like you've just been hugged by a Hallmark movie.

For more information visit her website, www.heathermiekstyn.com or follow her on Instagram @heathermiekstyn

ACKNOWLEDGEMENTS

First off, I want to thank my husband, Stephen. I could not have written this book without your support! Literally. If you hadn't put the kids to bed so often over the past few months, this book never would've happened. Not to mention, your skating skills inspired me to write this story in the first place. Thanks for being my happily ever after, babe.

Thanks so much to my four incredible girls. Even though most of the time you ask why I don't write books for kids, you are nonetheless always willing to provide me with a suggestion for a character's name or act out an expression I'm trying to describe. You even take ridiculous pictures of my feet for Instagram posts. And when you're all older, I hope you do read my books. Like, I REALLY hope you do. Seriously, if none of you become romance readers, I will cry. No pressure though.

A big thank you also to Meghan from Magic for Miles for the amazing cover! Girl, you are so talented! Sending you all the heart-eye emojis!

Thank you to Lindsey and Karalin for loving every book I send your way. I am so blessed by your friendship and encouragement! Love you both!

Thanks to my sister, Caitlin, who doesn't even usually read

romance, but still spent hours on the phone with me discussing not only this book, but every other book I've written. Thank you, also, to her son for being born, as her maternity leave was what allowed her to be home and available to me for all of these phone calls. Also, he's really cute and snuggly. So, he gets a shout-out for that too.

Thanks to my ARC readers and all of the lovely bookstagrammers who promoted my book for me or even just liked a post about it. People who read are simply the best.

A huge thanks to all my readers! It's fun to just write, but it's even more fun to have people who read what you write!

Shout-out also to my parents. You raised a reader. And I wouldn't be a writer without that foundation.

And lastly, thank you to my heavenly Father. What an amazing gift to be made in the image of my perfect creator. I can never thank you enough for everything you've done for me.

Printed in Great Britain
by Amazon